# THE MAN IN
# THE STRETCHER

previously uncollected short fiction by

## Kenneth Bernard

with an afterword by Harold Jaffe

STARCHERONE BOOKS / BUFFALO, NY

Also by Kenneth Bernard

*Night Club and other plays*
*Two Stories*
*The Maldive Chronicles* (fiction)
*How We Danced While We Burned ...* (plays)
*Curse of Fool* (plays)
*The Baboon in the Night Club* (poetry)
*Clown at Wall: A Kenneth Bernard Reader* (fiction,
      plays, poetry)
*From the District File* (fiction)
*The Magic Show of Dr. Ma-Gico* (play, in
      *Ridiculous Theatre*, ed. B. Marranca, G.
      Dasquest)
*The Qui-Parle Play & Poems*

# THE MAN IN THE STRETCHER

Kenneth Bernard

2005

Starcherone Books
PO Box 303
Buffalo, NY 14201
www.starcherone.com

©2005, by Kenneth Bernard

Grateful acknowledgment is made to the following periodicals, books, and anthologies where these fictions first appeared: *Asylum Annual*: "Antecedents." *Bennington Review*: "Thrift." *Chelsea Review*: "The War of the Footnotists and Endnotists. *Clown at Wall: A Kenneth Bernard Reader* (Conrontation Press, 1996): "Swallowing." *Concepts in Context: Aspects of the Writer's Craft* (ed. R. Kytel): "Lycanthrope." *Contre-Vox* (France): "Prolégomènes." *Crime Zone*: "Subway II, III." *Downtown Brooklyn*: "Chain-Saw," "News Story," "Umbrella Man," "Unspeakable Litanies, Impossible Act[ion]s," "Keeping a Log. *Fiction International*: "The Third Kiss, or Cobra Woman Meets the Bag Lady," "Prolegomena," "Nullity," "Book-Lending: A True Story," "Travel Guide," "My New Library." *Flash Fiction* (ed. James Thomas): "Vines." *Frank*: "Of Men and Dogs." *Harper's*: "Lycanthrope," "Reprieve." *Iowa Review*: "Columbus Day," "Eyes, Ears, Noses," "Vines." *MacGuffin*: "A Psycho-Metaphysical Fiction." *Minnesota Review*: "The Man in the Stretcher." *Le Moule à Gaufres* (France): "L'argent dans ma vie." *Mundus Artium*: The Man with the Beast in Him." *(New) American Review*: "The Queen of Moths." *Paris Review*: "For Irving: A Conversion." *Perishable Press*: "The War of the Footnotists and Endnotists," "Nullity." *Response: A Contemporary Jewish Review*: "Swallowing." *Salmagundi*: "The Dream of Writing in Arabic Script," "The Nasty Man," "Trimming Hedge," "Losing Ground," "Fish Eye," "Flâneur." *Tri-Quarterly*: "Subway I." *Two Stories*: "The Queen of Moths."

Text editor: Brandon Stosuy. Book editor: Ted Pelton. Cover design: Geoffrey Gatza. Cover collage: Kenneth Bernard. Proofreading: Florine Melnyk.

Library of Congress Cataloging-in-Publication Data

Bernard, Kenneth.
  The man in the stretcher : previously uncollected short fiction / by Kenneth Bernard ; with an afterword by Harold Jaffe.
    p. cm.
  ISBN 0-9703165-6-9 (pbk. : alk. paper)
  I. Title.

PS3552.E7264M36 2005
813'.54--dc22

2004026787

# TABLE OF CONTENTS

1. Swallowing — 11
2. The Nasty Man — 17
3. Book-Lending: A True Story — 23
4. Chain-Saw — 27
5. The Spider in the Tub — 32
6. Bats — 38
7. The Third Kiss, Or Cobra Woman Meets the Bag Lady — 46
8. The Money in My Life — 70
9. Trimming Hedge — 74
10. The Queen of Moths — 78
11. For Irving: A Conversion — 82
12. The Man with the Beast in Him — 90
13. Eyes, Ears, Noses — 94
14. Reprieve — 97
15. Antecedents — 100
16. A Psycho-Metaphysical Fiction — 106
17. Ex Facto Oritur Ius — 131
18. Vines — 135
19. Columbus Day — 138
20. Fish Eye — 141

| | |
|---|---|
| 21. Umbrella Man | 147 |
| 22. Of Men and Dogs | 151 |
| 23. Lycanthrope | 156 |
| 24. Keeping a Log | 159 |
| 25. Road-Kill | 163 |
| 26. Fly-Swat | 166 |
| 27. The Dream of Writing in Arabic Script | 174 |
| 28. Travel Guide | 177 |
| 29. Flâneur | 188 |
| 30. The War of the Footnotists and Endnotists | 195 |
| 31. My New Library | 201 |
| 32. Subway I, II, III | 209 |
| 33. Impossible Litanies, Necessary Act[ion]s | 216 |
| 34. News Story | 222 |
| 35. A Few Words, a Little Shelter | 226 |
| 36. Prolegomena | 230 |
| 37. Thrift | 237 |
| 38. Losing Ground | 239 |
| 39. Nullity | 242 |
| 40. The Man in the Stretcher | 251 |

*Afterword: The Man with the Beast in Him,*
   *by Harold Jaffe*     279

For Katey and Jack, Marlon and Malcolm

# SWALLOWING

I was telling my son recently of a most interesting natural phenomenon I once witnessed. Two tropical snakes (I must write of my travels one day) were locked in mortal combat. Their manner of combat was to press into one another, open mouth to open mouth, until one managed to overlap the other. Then began the slow forcing shut of one snake's mouth and his disappearance, inch by inch, into the other until only one bulging snake remained. My interest, of course, is with the swallowed one. I already know most of the sensations of swallowing, even of live things, like jungle cockroaches. But I know nothing of the sensations of being swallowed. And who would want to? you quite correctly say. Well, let's say it is an academic interest. After all, most of creation at one time or another experiences the sensation of being swallowed. How do they feel about it? I realize that a snake has a very small brain. But what about a zebra? The zebra is not of such lowly proportion. What does the still quivering zebra think when the lion is already feasting on its exposed entrails? And even the snake must experience some sensation. I hope it is not necessary to multiply my examples. For example, the frog plucked up by the crane in one swift gulp, or the serenely swimming duck dragged down into the murky depths by the snapping turtle. It is an area of exploration that has been overlooked by science and philosophy. And it is difficult to understand why. It is, after all, a unique sensation, a sudden ceasing to be for the sake of becoming something else. Horrible as it is, I suppose it is a reincarnation of a sort, even a kind of immortality. Perhaps in the creatures swallowed there is some such awareness that at the final moments makes it all right. Certainly in most creatures there comes a moment when struggle is suspended, when, though not yet ceasing to be the thing they were, they are already resigned to becoming a new thing. When only the legs of a frog stick out from the snake's mouth, they do not kick very convincingly. Perhaps it is comparable to the feeling of human creatures in their last moments when the murmur of prayer eases their passage because of its immortal inference. I realize that someone might object to the comparison. But I cannot help it. I suppose I have a kind of swallowing, of being-swallowed, complex. I cannot really feel, and I do not believe, that in this so universal of experiences the human creature is left out. Certainly I am not. To say that we are all swallowed by death would be sophistry, for so is all life swallowed by death. But a frog is also swallowed by a snake. Wherein are we so swallowed? That is my question. There is, I suppose, some suitability in the example of the Jews and the gas chambers. But were the Jews swallowed by the gas chambers or by the Germans? And into what further life were they swallowed? They certainly did not make the gas chambers fatter, though admittedly one could argue that in one way or another they made the Germans fatter. It is an idea with a certain amount of charm. In every German there is a swallowed Jew. Have you never seen a German with the legs of a Jew sticking out of his mouth? I don't mean to be facetious. I am most serious about the matter. Sometimes at night I wake up and experience a frightening sensation of constriction. My bed, my furniture, the walls of my apartment, the very city I live in close in on me. At such moments I would not dare to rouse my wife for comfort. Her mouth would be enormous, and I should not even resist. I just lie there and try to control my breathing and my heart beat. I think of open fields and flowers and sunlight. I remember the times I have played with my son and how much he needs me, how much there is in the world that would terrify him were I not there to explain it to him. A comforting thought has just occurred to me. In the act of getting buried we are in fact swallowed by the earth. And from the earth we, too, spring again into other lives. Perhaps that is why we make such a ritual of it, no matter what we believe. We have an abiding, though unrecognized, faith in the efficacy of being swallowed, even going so far as to bury our ashes. Perhaps this the closest we can come to the frog that has ceased to kick. It signifies our humility before the mystery of life and death, before God.

And it is a most bearable swallowing. We are such powerful creatures on this earth, anyway, that what is there but the earth itself that could swallow us? Yes, I know your thought; there is my example of the Germans. But why, then, pick on the Germans? What does it mean, to give you another example, that it is everywhere a sign of manhood to eat your meat rare, even raw? Is it not true that women love men who swallow living things more than men who do not ask? Ask any woman whether she would marry a vegetarian. Most of them will smile, without knowing why. And to be sure, some of them *would* marry vegetarians. But what kind of women are they? So you understand what I mean? It would seem that we have cut ourselves off from one of nature's central realities. We all *aspire* to the condition of swallowing things, but we have for various reasons inhibited this aspiration. Hence the excessive importance we give to those few expressions of this aspiration that we allow. Men have divorced women who could not cook their meat properly. Give them *well done* when they have asked for *rare* and their entire self-image is threatened. Chopped meat is a sign of impotence because it does not retain the form of its original source, hence it is far removed from the image of man swallowing a living thing. I am well aware that there is a whole sociology to be built on this insight. There are infinite ramifications, for example the existence of the being-swallowed within the swallowing. But I leave that and other matters to more subtle minds than mine. Let us take, for a moment, the execution of criminals. We either shoot them, electrocute them, choke them, or gas them. Elsewhere they behead, crucify, and impale them. And no doubt there are refinements I've never heard of. These acts, whether public or not, arouse universal interest. And this is because they are a civilized expression of the aspiration to swallow living things. They are, so to speak, raw meat. Granted these men must be exterminated, are there not more humane ways? Would it not, for example, be far more humane to have each man alone with his mode of execution and let him do it in his own good time? Thus would we remove most of the horrible sense of being swallowed which comes from our rigid adherence to form, but nonetheless retain the swallowing. Imagine a man and his electric chair. He reads in it, he eats in it, he rests in it, he thinks in it. Perhaps it is even his potty. He comes to know it and to be comfortable with it. One day he gives himself a little shock just to see what it is like. He is surprised. Just a slight burning sensation, a momentary paralysis. Not at all what he expected. He fiddles with it for weeks, even months, until he has endured quite severe shocks. But they are *his* shocks. He is in control. One day, not at all because he planned it, he turns on the power more than he has ever done before. Without realizing it he has passed the point of no return because his body is powerless to respond. The burning and paralysis increase and he yields to the inevitable.

Soon he is dead. Perhaps he even smiles during the process because of an accomplishment well done. In dying and subsequently being buried he has been swallowed into eternity. And in dying by the prescribed mode, electrocution, he has been swallowed by that corporate entity, society, that is, ourselves. Of course there is pain—but it is a thoroughly familiar pain, and he brought it upon himself. Humane? Obviously. But just as obviously impossible. Why? Because there would be insufficient swallowing; we would not have a sufficient sense of the frog going down. Perhaps you think I go too far, digress really. After all, there has been a tremendous jump somewhere. People are not snakes. True, very true. But how then do you explain my dread of being swallowed? I assure you I live with it more each day. I am wary of neighbors. I look into people's plates when they eat. I tremble sometimes when I see them chew. What do we really know about houses of slaughter anyway? Where are they? Who works in them? You see, you hesitate, you don't know. And now you laugh. Are you listening to your laugh? I assure you I am quite sane and a most productive member of this society. I am a classic example of the family man. I need rest, but there is no place to get it. Needless to say I have not discussed all this with my son. I have limited myself to a factual description of the two writhing snakes. But obviously I shall have to tell him. Yes, someday he will have to know.

## THE NASTY MAN

If I were to say that the rectum is the ultimate hiding place, who knows what people would think of me? That is not how you make philosophy. Yet it is true. When we are very young we seek to hoard everything there. Life is as perfect as it can be for us, having been born. We yield our perfect capital only reluctantly, and when we capitulate totally, conceding ourselves to the vast plumbing of society and civilization, we feel thereafter a core of loss. As we say, we grow up, we become citizens of life and reality, feebly making our way. But a certain dream of wholeness lives on, in myth, story, and song. Often what we appear to do is but the mask of something else. We appear to be busy little bankers and dentists and Indian chiefs, but in fact we are secretly busy trying to stuff the world back into our original hiding place. I first began to notice this in small ways. For example, slots. I realized one day that I was taking inordinate pleasure in putting coins or tokens in slots, cards in slits, checks in envelopes. In banks, my hand sliding carefully over counters and under grills, through Plexiglas apertures, became erotic; and sex itself, with its deposits and withdrawals, various accruals and maturations, became banking. Paper bags, wallets, purses, closets, cellars, attics, tool boxes, picnic lunches, socks, cars, creels, dressers, *eating* (eating perhaps above all), keys and keyholes—a thousand immediate things—became a means of redressing my original loss, of putting back what I had so rudely been dispossessed of. Of course, such efforts, such alchemy, even when obsessional, is doomed to failure. Once out, some things cannot be put back. We lose our sense of wholeness early. And that loss, that continuing loss, gives a tragical cast of our lives and accounts for a certain messiness in human affairs, a certain scrambling that is the very nature of things.

Now of course one can say that this does not seem to be an uplifting philosophy of life. It is like telling someone to eat rotten cabbage. To this I answer that I am not interested in philosophies of life but rather in life. And as I look at life, from small things to large, from piggy banks to our great genocidal incorporations, it seems to me to be an attempt to perfect the imperfectible, to stuff back into our secret place what we were stripped of at an early age. In various states of rage, people are frenetically engaged towards this single impossible goal, and to the degree that such actions create a social hum we can say that here we have life, here we have community, here indeed we have civilization. Obviously, I am ill-suited to be a member of it. I have too twitchy a nose, for one thing. There is hardly an esthetics to be made from my observations. And yet, in my own fashion, that is indeed what I am after, an esthetics of life, something that moves forward in mutilated joy rather than backwards in rage. And to achieve it I can see that I must be a revolutionary, an outcast, a crackpot, a nasty person even.

It appears people must be aware of this. Let me describe one or two recurring situations. People do talk to me, but less and less. I always listen very attentively, but not particularly to what they are saying. No. For what they think they are saying is not what they are really saying. I discount all noise that has as its end an amassing of life for their secret place. There is always a smell to it. No, I seek rather to respond to any bell-like sound or any act that reflects something freely given, some small bit of life there for others' taking, a throwing off, come what will. Consequently, I think I might have a vacant, disconcerting look, a withholding aspect, the cast of assent not given. In the far distance of my look there is, I think, a laughter and a scorn. People, I fear, feel naked somehow, feel caught in the act of stuffing things in their secret places. And they become, briefly, embarrassed, then angry. For this is a supreme private act, however transparent. How dare I look. Perhaps if people would practice viewing themselves in a mirror, with a finger poked into their secret place, they might learn something, unstopper themselves and then see *me* in a better perspective. But it is not an epistemology likely to be followed.

Nor am I likely to be embraced by my fellow man in the near future.

Another thing I do is to help people amass for their secret place. This is a good example of my nastiness. Properly translated, most people are saying, "I am really quite wonderful" or "How right and proper it was to have acted and spoken as I did." I no longer argue with such sentiments. (Better to look to ants for altruism than any Organization for the Betterment of Mankind). Rather, I say, "Indeed you are quite wonderful. You are, in fact, a saint." And, "I agree entirely. You should have kicked your mother down *three* flights of steps, not two." You can see my point. Give people what they want and they will only smell all the more. Dead bodies everywhere. After a while, I give people the uncomfortable feeling that someone else's fingers are helping to stuff things in their secret places—money, awards for virtue, sausages, automobiles even. There is no limit. And that spoils something for them. Again the feeling of nakedness. And the rage. Nothing is worse than someone else putting sweets in one's rectum. It is imperative that certain actions appear to be innocent and unrecognized for what they are. How else would we avoid laughing to tears when others professed to us? "My dear woman, won't you simply look at where your fingers are? Do you not see the poor Ubangi's head sticking out?" The difficulty, often, is that some people appear to be amassing for good and decent ends. How dare you look vacant when I tell you how many starving mouths I have filled, what programs I have fomented for the elevation of men and women everywhere? One must not be deceived. There are more ways than one to skin a savage.

    Now you might well argue that this is the very *nature* of civilization, to amass for the secret place rather than a letting loose, a freely and happily yielding to the world's plumbing. And I will answer two things possibly. First, is there only this one civilization? Are there not those who give without this contamination? And second, cannot things be changed? Are we doomed by our language and by the circumstances of our history? Must we bloat ourselves until we explode? Of course, another question is hardly an answer. Perhaps more questions are only evasions. Perhaps one would have to be, say, a cockroach to be more giving, more dispersing. And perhaps happy Watusi soiling the plain is mere sentimentality. No doubt. And, after all, although the world might be in serious decline, it is *very successfully* in serious decline. Things *work*. We have magnificent edifices and enterprises within which we work and take our pleasures. We have *recorded* and *analyzed* our progress. We know exactly where we are and have proclaimed the good of it. We are, by and large, handsome and good people, well anointed, increasingly with better teeth, displayed everywhere. But we are also bloated. We have taken back into us what we never wanted to give. And the bloat spreads.

True reality has yet to explode on us. And out of the muck, what creature will arise?

## BOOK-LENDING: A TRUE STORY

Some years ago I lent a book to a colleague. It was a book about a terrible time, written by a Polish Aryan who had spent several nightmare years in camps whose business was killing. After the war, he stuck his head in an oven and died. I was moved by the book, by the irony, the upsidedowness of its world. My colleague, struck by my description of the book, asked to borrow it. I was reluctant but did not show my reluctance to him. I thought, maybe he is really interested; maybe he is imagining what might have been his fate had he not been born of immigrants. I had once been friendly with my colleague. But one day, in the midst of a friendly debate, I realized that he did not really believe what he was saying, that he never had. He fancied himself a kind of philosopher-king, albeit insufficiently heralded, and took any side of an argument, usually opposite to yours, to display his logical skills, which were considerable. Truth did not interest him. From that moment, I ceased my relationship, except for formalities. I am not much of a debater. To have my views entangled and then demolished in what was, after all, only a game, was more than I was willing to endure. Even blood, for him, was never human, merely a debating point. No doubt he would have been an excellent survivor, but not one to put his head in an oven. So I worried about my book. Although I had read it, I missed not having it in my possession. Several years after, when our encounters had considerably cooled and I thought a reasonable amount of time had passed, I asked about the book. He said he had returned it. I was stunned, more than stunned, but again I said nothing. Perhaps he believed he had returned it. I don't know. I am fairly sure he did not read it. Certainly he had never mentioned it. What I think happened is this. When I first mentioned the book, he had a momentary philosopher-king interest in it and asked to borrow it. Then he promptly forgot about it, and it sank into oblivion among his possessions. It is possible, I suppose, that he did read it, or part of it, but it presented a conflict for him. What could he debate? His solution was subtle: clean hands, but no book. Point scored. In any event, there was nothing I could do. In later years, he found some causes and pursued them relentlessly, ruthlessly even, to no good end. Partly, I think this was because he had been chosen, briefly, for higher office, but he had been found wanting. His wisdom, or his craftiness, was not appreciated, and he was returned to his former position. His causes became a kind of revenge. Then he became ill, underwent drastic surgeries, lingered on a few years as elder statesman to a clique of younger colleagues, and finally retired to a plantation-like setting for old people.

Now all of this is mere background. For I was still missing my book. Although it will seem mad, I confess that for me his worst transgression was his "disappearance" of my book. He had managed to make several million people and untold suffering disappear. And for what? What was his final score? I am sorry he is suffering and probably dying, but who is not? There is always something in the manner of it. Sometimes I imagine that a package will arrive in the mail. It will be the book. No note, just the book. It would make all the difference in the world to me. Or, I should say, it would have, because I now have another copy. My wife, to whom I have spoken about this matter over the years, decided to make a new copy an anniversary present. And I am rereading it. Today I read, "Right after the boxing match I took in another show—I went to hear a concert. Over in Birkenau you could probably never imagine what feats of culture we are exposed to here, just a few kilometers away from the smoldering chimneys." And again:

> Despite the madness of war, we lived for a world that would be different. For a better world to come when all this is over. And perhaps even our being here is a step toward that world. Do you really think that, without the hope that such a world is possible, that the rights of man will be restored again, we could stand the concentration camp, even for a day? It is that very hope that makes people go without a murmur to the gas chambers, keeps

them from risking a revolt, paralyzes them into numb inactivity. It is a hope that breaks down family ties, makes mothers renounce their children, or wives sell their bodies for bread, or husbands kill… We were never taught how to give up hope and this is why today we perish in gas chambers.

It all seems fresh and new to me. I deeply regret the loss of the young man who wrote that. Or who wrote, "…I like to think that one day we shall have the courage to tell the truth by its proper name." Before he was thirty and ended his life, he did manage to tell the truth by its proper name. It was in the book I lent and never got back. It was in the book that was never acknowledged. My wise wife has repaired what she could. Reading it again has been good for me. Some things are not debatable. There is one odd thing, however. The print of this copy is all aslant, out of alignment with the cut pages. Philosophically I can accept that, but I know there are no philosophers left in publishing. Is this another act of disappearance? I don't know. I have written for another copy.

## CHAIN-SAW

Let me tell you about my chain-saw. First of all, it terrifies me, even though it is only sixteen inches. The bar, I mean, on which the cutting chain rotates. You see, not only have I heard many horrible stories of what this instrument can do, particularly from the old man who sold it to me and who services it for me, but also I have lost my gloves, my thick protective gloves, which just might save me a finger, should the occasion arise. And that is a story in itself. The old man who sold me the chain-saw also sold me the gloves. I suspected that he might be fooling me, that no real wielder of a chain-saw used gloves, and even if he did, they would not be so expensive and bulky as mine. But I could not, in my ignorance, afford to overlook any barrier between me and injury. At first I kept the gloves and the chain-saw together, even when I left my chain-saw with a neighbor for the winter, which I had to do because we have been robbed many times in the off seasons. That is still another story. At any rate, this last winter (when, thank god, we were *not* robbed), I inadvertently kept the gloves and returned with them to the city. At least I think I did. I have vague memories of seeing them out of context and wondering where I might have put them so as to be certain I reunited them with the saw when the time came. But perhaps, foreseeing their placelessness in the city, I hid them, as I do many other things, on the farm. My problem is twofold. First, as I have said, my chain-saw terrifies me. Second, I cannot find the gloves which just might save me a finger or two. This has prompted all sorts of thoughts, which I shall try to list (and limit):

1. If I should lose a finger, whose fault would it be?

2. Did the old man, a long-time logger, who sold me the chain-saw, lie to me about the value of using the gloves? There is, after all, a certain clumsiness in using them. Does that clumsiness create its own kind of danger?

3. I have seen chain-saw users without fingers. I often imagine the swift moment of contact and the bright spurting blood. At that moment, did they know what they were looking at? Should I ask them whether or not they wore gloves?

4. Who are the people who rob me and why do they do it? (Are any of them fingerless?) It is because of their depredations that I have misplaced my gloves. (Is that really true?) But they are faceless. Even should they smile upon seeing my stump, I could not wave it in their faces in anger. (But why not? Even were they innocent of direct involvement in the chain of events leading to the loss of a finger, might not they be in secret or unknowing *collusion*

with the perpetrators?)

5. Who are the "perpetrators"?

6. *Why do I consider the gloves out of context in the city? Am I similarly out of context on the farm?* Considering the many unanswerable questions in this matter, and the possible consequences, can we ask whether or not it is perhaps in the nature of things that we are all out of context, one way or another? For example, would one of my robbers stick out like an amputated thumb in the city? Might he, also for example, be directed in jest to dangerous areas, just as I was directed to buy the gloves? Finally, does the chain-saw have a "mind" and destiny of its own, which I (we) cannot perceive? It is not, after all, a sudden miraculous appearance on the earth. Might not lopped fingers and gashed throats have been centuries in the making?

7. Did I pay too much for the gloves? How can I possibly know what too much is?

8. Was I guilty of hubris in buying the chain-saw? Did I *deserve* the chain-saw? Had I *earned* it? What, after all, do I know about the inner workings of a chain-saw?

9. What, exactly, *is* a chain-saw?

10. What, for that matter, is a finger?

11. I am convinced that whoever robs me feels no guilt.

12. I speak of the possibility of my gloves saving me a finger, should the occasion arise. What is the occasion? Why does it sound strangely like an opportunity? Is the opportunity to save or to lose a finger? Are the gloves thereby good or bad? What is the context?

13. I also speak of reuniting my gloves with my chain-saw when the time came. What time am I speaking of? What is the real task at hand? What is to be confirmed, proven, tested, *done*? Would I be making a fatal mistake to use the gloves? Or not to use them?

14. Finally (?), it is clear to me that one story is always part of other stories. In that sense, no story can ever be complete. To be sure, something always happens in a story, but so much more does not happen. In short, all stories lop off fingers. All stories are like chain-saws. For example, they lop off *connections* also. This bothers me. Should it?

As you can see, increasingly I feel I am a character in a drama I do not understand. Nor do I understand my role. Am I tragic, am I comic? Am I simply background, a walk-on, and if so, for what? Who are the main characters? (Is the chain-saw one? Is the bloody stump one?) Now, of course, I might attempt some resolution by giving my chain-saw away, or selling it, or keeping it but not using it. But sooner or later I will discover the gloves. *Where* I find them will, of course, be revealing. What I do *because* of finding them will also be revealing. At the moment, I have all of my fingers. (Do I have all of everything else?) Nevertheless, I frequently fantasize that one of them is missing. I put myself in various situations, without my finger. It is an entirely different, alternate, life. (How many such lives do I have?) Oddly, this is giving me a certain amount of comfort. But there is a disquieting note. What if, instead of a finger, I were contemplating the loss of a hand? Or an arm?… Is that still another story? Another life? How far can such a story or life go? I don't know. I don't want to know.

## THE SPIDER IN THE TUB

There is no question that *things* are in an unrecognized conspiracy to undo us. *Things* are constantly getting between us and our ends. Sometimes we trip on a shoelace and fall under a truck. A shoelace we took the trouble to tie well. Sometimes in putting on our pants they stick, our foot halfway down, and we rip a seam, or trip, crack our head, go insane, and leave three starving children. Things roll out of reach, even out of sight. Retrieving them we twist our back or neck, we hit our head, we pinch our finger, we get a sliver under our nail. Who can really deny that there is a conspiracy, that *things* are in league to defeat our purposes? They only *appear* to follow our laws. Round things roll, poor eye-hand coordination misdirects hammers, lesser force yields to greater force, and so on and on and on. But in the end, our laws give us no solace, no real happiness, no safety, for things always outstrip them. Why do we not recognize this? Is there not perhaps some deeper "logic" to the behavior of things? Do we not perhaps, without laws, our categories, our labels, put too smiling a face on things and consequently on life? Thereby blinding us to what is truly an unfathomable conspiracy? The question has not been phrased with sufficient force. We have yet to understand the legislators of things.

Tallying up my various encounters with things recently, I was moved to consider some *pro tem* counter-measures, some activity, necessary fictions, to restore my sense of security and purpose. It was not, you understand, some paranoid frenzy I was contemplating, but rather a simple recognition of a network beyond my comprehension. Take, for example (and isn't that suddenly a quaint phrase, as if anything could ever, really, be an example?), the ripped trousers above. There are so many things that might be said about them. Let me list some:

1. Perhaps it is the first beautiful day of spring (or your birthday or your anniversary) and you wish to savor every moment of it. Hence you rush, misplacing your foot, or losing your balance or timing, or miscalculating the force of your thrust.

2. Or it is raining for the fourth, fifth, or twentieth day and that disgruntles you.

3. Or you have finished a shower but not wiped your feet adequately because you are increasingly prone to a stiff back in the morning because of a new mattress your wife bought from your despised brother-in-law. And when you put your foot in the trouser leg, your foot catches because of the dampness—

4.   Or you have not cut your toenails because the nail clipper is not where it is supposed to be. And one nail is split and you—

5.   Or your wife calls you at just that moment to ask what date it is or what you have done with the nail clipper or what homunculoid fantasy is—

6.   Or you see a spider in the tub, something you have never seen and never expected to see. A little thought here will reveal to you the importance of seeing this, the spider in the tub, as a sign in a new language, which you have not learned because you have not recognized it as such.

Now thus far we are speaking only of the *leg in the trouser* (enormous enough) and we have, so to speak, only scratched the surface of things. There is far more to say than has been said. Let us say your leg *does* go through. Perhaps the trouser leg *is* ripped. Perhaps you *do* crack your head. Perhaps you merely (*Merely*? By what right is anything *merely*?) rip the nail off, bleed, later limp and—Can we possibly exhaust the ramifications of any one of them? Why were not the trouser legs wider? A thousand words at least. Why were you not more careful? Ten thousand words. What epic lies behind your uncut nails and the missing clipper? Who can possibly have such knowledge of society or the psyche or the body—*or the trousers themselves*, with their millions of threads, their seams, their folds, their socioeconomic history? And at the fingertips constantly? The thing to remember is that disaster is implicit in *everything* at every moment and we can never *calculate* the permutations of it. This recognition achieved, we must then deal with the horror of it all, the darkness that always lies in wait, the terrible holocaust things constantly threaten us with, to which we have been blind, utterly blind.

Of course, perfect stasis is the perfect solution. But not possible in this game of life. So we need therapeutic exercises, strategies, some means of establishing a working sense of confidence. For example, we can practice knocking a pin off the table. Here again, of course, there is the specter of the cracked head and a ruined life. *Why* do pins get swept off tables? We cannot really answer that. A million words would not suffice. What we can do, however, is *deliberately* knock the pin off the table, ten, thirty, a hundred times. (Our libraries do little more than that.) And having knocked the pin off the table, never once lunging for it, never worrying where it has disappeared to, never losing patience with getting on our hands and knees again, looking and feeling like idiots. And if it totally *disappears*? That is not the worst consideration. True concentration on things always leads to their disappearance. Although there is no question that this exercise confers a measure of confidence, there is naturally a dark corner, even after a thousand repetitions, after, so to speak, civilization has staked its claim. Practice is never a rehearsal (and rehearsal itself is a delusion). Let us make the table edge the edge of a cliff, and the pin some cherished object, good, or person. It does not matter whether the cliff is real or metaphoric, the point is still the same: there will come a time, *any* time, when we will, *must*, lunge, for if we do not, something will be irretrievably lost. And once we lunge—then we are back to the trousers. Who can answer for what will happen? *Things* take over. And we simply have not considered things enough. Even when we have at least taken thoughtful note of them, when we have perhaps practiced to *contain* things, tried our trousers a thousand times, we still cannot call the consequences. Something can always go over the cliff, and we, in lunging to save it (*Why*? *Why*?), throw ourselves into chaos. This is when we should begin to regard the language of the spider in the tub more closely. For the spider speaks to us when we despair over the cracking of our heads. And what does the spider say? Words cannot uncover this. What can *I* say? Respect ye the power of *things* in your life? Blind not yourself to the hidden realm beneath your thumb? *Things* weave conspiracies our language, our systems, our history cannot contain? And when, fully trousered, you lie bleeding on the floor, open your mind, open your heart, and tremble?—Perhaps. Trembling for the life that lies in wait is always a good idea. It subverts homeostasis (O dew-lipp'd glen, where have you gone?) More practical, I think, is to mull certain words and phrases that metaphorically crop up without our seeing them. For example, from above, other than the very important spider in the tub, consider:

1. The leg in the trouser.
2. So to speak.
3. At the fingertips.
4. Game of life.
5. Undo.
6. For example (of course).
7. The stiff back in the morning, e.g., the snapping turtle in the pond (we all swim naked): winter equals respite.
8. The surface of things.
9. Scratching the surface of things.
10. Solution.

These will take one a far distance. The question is where, and then why where will never do. Lists are endless, and we must learn to thank somebody, or some thing, for that.

# BATS

Last night there was a bat in our bedroom. Don't make too much of that. Our cat was very excited. It was his first bat. It was not, however, our first bat. My wife immediately put on a wide-brimmed garden hat and armed herself with a broom. I, alternatively, opened the screens, put out the lights, and shut the door, persuading her to sleep elsewhere. A good solution, it turned out. Bats in the bedroom are notoriously hard to hit with a broom. Don't make too much of that either.

I must have dreamed a bit about the bat because I woke up before the dawn with some hazy thoughts about it. First of all, how the bat got into the bedroom, or the house, for that matter, is a complete mystery. One Easter, tracing down a foul smell, we eventually found a dead mallard duck, caked with the blood it had shed trying to escape. How the mallard got in is also a mystery, for the house is shut tight for the winter. I have not thought too much about the duck (until just now, that is), but I have given the bat considerable thought. Let me say right away that I know that a complete and methodical investigation would most likely reveal how the bat got into the bedroom. But it would not explain why.

It never does. Second, if we did not kill the bat with the broom, or something else, and if we did not open a window and screen, the bat would flutter around forever, or at least for a bat life. Outside the window is its natural realm, near and far at the same time. Inside the window is an unnatural realm (few insects, for example), and no amount of fluttering will help. Of course, it is possible (but unlikely) that a bat will exit a house as mysteriously as it entered. But even with the window and screen open it is not certain (although it is likely) that the bat will exit. Now a bat, of course, for various complicated reasons (not to be gone into here), arouses a degree of panic. When there is a bat in the bedroom, something needs to be done to restore calm and equilibrium, to make for peaceful sleep. The question is what, and how. I have a number of observations on this matter:

1. Foremost is something visual—the nearness of the bat to its natural environment and the importance of what we might call a "window of opportunity." We all, in a sense, need open windows, or at least the inclination to open one when some occasion requires it. The drawback, of course, is that just as some things can go out of windows, so too other things can come in. Open windows bring different worlds close together. What if, for example, a bat goes out but an owl comes in? And so on. Well, one might suggest that we can get used to bats and owls, but that

would require an entirely new approach to our panic, and probably some other things, like history, or philosophy. Of course, we could simply apply the broom approach and kill all intruders and check all our windows and screens, all our chinks. However, that will never take care of the totally *mysterious* entry of a bat, or something else. Perhaps that can be tolerated. Some degree of panic might be acceptable and even useful, for example, in our imaginative life, in our art, in our dreams. Not all people agree with this.

2. Why do I claim that it is unlikely that the bat will exit the house as mysteriously as it entered? Probably because I feel the permutations of its entry are limitless, and the permutations that allowed it entry are unlikely, especially in reverse, to be repeated in this world. What particular insect had it pursued (and after how many others?), how many flutters of its wing-like appendages, how many twists and turns, what design, which invisible aperture (and for how long a time), what configuration of millions of creatures and millions of stars? That is merely the outside. What of the inside? More millions of permutations. What is this new and strange realm (with us in it) accomplishing, moment by moment, in the bat? Can we really call it a bat any longer, once it is inside? (What would we be if *we* went "outside"?)

3.   Why do I say it is likely (but not certain), with the window and screen open, that the bat will exit? First of all, although I have no solid grounds for saying this, the bat will very likely wish to remain a bat. It has no doubts about its essence. Its best hope of remaining a bat is to return quickly to its natural realm, and if there is a window of opportunity to do so it will likely take it. The longer it neglects the open window, the less it will be a bat. That is partly why I say "but not certain." If it ceases enough to be a bat, it might do strange things, like flying into walls, or other, less predictable things. Even in the best of circumstance, a bat might not exit. There is no explanation for that. Some bats never leave. Killing the bat at that point does not necessarily get rid of it. Something has failed. But, also, something new might have come into being. What? And whether good or bad for us is difficult to say.

4.   I refer several times to killing a bat, with a broom "or something else." What is the something else? What is the proper method of killing a bat? A poison spray? A meat cleaver? Trapping or drowning? Each method presents interesting problems. For example, I undoubtedly would be changed, but differently, depending on my choice. In fact, there is, as yet, no proper method for killing a bat. That is probably because there is no rationale either. With a rationale, we can often discover a proper

method. Slitting throats, for example.

All of this brings me to "bats in the belfry," a phrase I have not appreciated enough. I am not unaware of a certain religious denotation to the phrase. After all, a belfry is a tower, often a bell tower, and bell towers are usually associated with churches, which seems very proper. But an earlier use denotes warfare. Any moveable tower used to storm enemy walls may be called a belfry. Now "bats in the belfry," I would say, is very much limited to church towers these days, although perhaps something of the earlier implications of warfare, of conflict, remain. The thing about bats in a church tower is that they obviously come and go freely. The church seems to live quite easily with bats in its belfry. However, when the phrase is applied to a person, it is more the idea of the bat locked in the bedroom. There is no egress. Something is awry. For better or worse, we are not like churches; our towers are sealed. In this situation, when a bat gets in, a person becomes unpredictable, flying into walls, so to speak. This, I suppose, is a way of saying that bedrooms (or houses) should be more like belfries, that is, open to entrance and egress, although even if so, there are, as I have said, no guarantees: the bats might never leave; a person might need to be locked up, or isolated, or subjected to a meat cleaver. Also, there are no "bells" in bedrooms, at least any more, to summon people to worship things beyond their ken, or at least to promote a tolerance of such things. We like to build our houses tight. That is our suitable realm, such as it is. Nevertheless, there is always the chance that one might inexplicably discover, say, a brightly-colored mallard duck behind a trunk to provoke some odd thoughts or acts. Hermetic and rational as houses are, bats will get in, and other things. How one deals with such exigencies is not the least important matter of how one deals with what is called a life. It would, of course, be foolish to conclude too much on the basis of all this. One should probably be slow to define what a house is, how it should be constructed, and so on. For example, is a house a fortress? Is it a refuge? What action is going on? And why? One might, however, in conclusion, venture these few words. Be aware of windows and screens and what they connect. Be aware of what can come in and what can go out. Above all, do not place complete faith in windows, however used, or in screens, or in houses, however well built. There is always something else.

Afternote:

I am troubled by my reference to "a degree of panic" aroused by bats and my deferral of the issue. An eminent critic, in a reference to the comic strip character Batman, says that he is a "benignly Americanized version of the dark prince of Transylvania," who "fights an endless series of mutant, schizoid criminals by night."

But there is a difference. It is interesting to note that our humanoid version of the bat is a force for good and the Old World's version (*Nosferatu*) is an impregnable source of evil. But Batman, in taking the form (a bat) and the element (darkness) of primal evil to fight that evil, becomes himself dysfunctional as societal man. That is, he is like the bat who ceases to be a bat when too long confused in the bedroom. He has lost his natural element and, aside from a solitary boy companion (Robin, a bird of daylight), exists in lonely isolation, much like other mythic American battlers of evil. The truth of the matter is that Batman *should* succumb to the forces he battles, for he never admits their fundamental power. The renowned Bram Stoker does not make the same mistake in his novel. His Dracula is triumphant only as long as his opponents adhere to the structure of Enlightenment propositions (like science) and refuse to admit his existence. But once—against all reason—they do admit his existence, they succeed and drive a stake through his heart. The question of other vampires and their realm and purpose is left quite open, as it should be. Darkness is the elemental fostering condition of all the anxieties and fears we have about what resides outside our well-structured houses. In that darkness live all the creatures we struggle to keep out. Batman's "mutant, schizoid criminals" are like the creatures who have somehow, mistakenly, gotten in. The question is how to deal with them. A more troubling question is, as I think I have suggested earlier, whether or not we really do have protections, and if not, what can we do about it. I don't know. That great architects of our "protections" must surely be fooling us because in our better moments we know it is foolish to feel safe. Our eminent critic's use of "endless" above is in this respect quite right. Yet our society constructs ever more complicated structures precisely to convince us (in the service of what?) that safety is an attainable fact, even if we must endure the spectacle of various deranged heroes in that attainment littering the landscape. The true fact is that safety is a broom waving in the air. And my wife knows something of the efficacy of such a broom.

# THE THIRD KISS, OR
# COBRA WOMAN MEETS THE BAG LADY

Now the really interesting thing about cobras is their smell. Of course you will say who ever gets close enough to a cobra to smell it, except maybe a dead cobra. And a dead cobra smells of dead cobra. I'm speaking of the live, undulating cobra of the beady dark eyes and the darting tongue and the fangs folded inward so cunningly. Who has smelled that cobra? Well, of course there are the professional snake handlers of zoos and circuses, whose business it is to be in cobra's proximity. And sometimes, too, they pay the penalty for their familiarity and ignorance, mistaking routine for docility, that great error of civilization. And they die like sudden clowns, unable to breathe, or their hearts stopping with a stab. What a terrible consciousness must be theirs in those final moments, so knowing and so mute. Then there are those few of the scientific community who experiment with cobras and their ilk, extracting information or poison for the common good. But their noses do not work. They are stopped up. Formaldehyde is their true ether. They are also blind and clubfooted. A not so occasional Indian villager smells cobra, of course. Working in the wood or field, he kicks or lifts a harmless bark or tussock and from beneath it rises a worm of uncommon strength and length, dancing in front of him, confronting him outrageously with his destiny. He is quite naturally afraid to move. He thinks that if he is still, if he edges back by infinitesimal spaces, he can put himself beyond its deadly reach. But in truth, so overwhelmed is he by the enormity of the serpentine erection before him, so entangled is he in the deep musk smell oozing from every pore of its sleek skin, and, yes, so entranced is he by the beauty, the horrible foreign beauty, of the creature that has erupted from seemingly nowhere, that he does not know whether he is moving at all, does not even know anymore what movement is. He is benumbed as well as bedazzled by a new dimension of time and space. He hums, he throbs, he aches with it. And the cobra does not bother with micro-inches or millimeters. It knows the thought of movement before it even becomes movement. And so the villager, enthralled even as he loosens his sphincter, loosens everything, fouling the heavy air he was learning to love even as its initial bitterness appalled him, knows rather than feels the timeless kiss of cobra, and then the swift paralysis, rooted to the experience, cut off so totally from his world. *He* knows the smell of cobra, but whom can he tell?

    That leaves the famous fakir or marketplace and square with his cobra in a basket and his flute to lure her out. The drama, like the cobra, is small scale, and the music is mere diversion. But the crowds still gather. It is an enactment that fascinates, even though they know his swaying body is the key and that he has trained since youth on the bites of baby cobras. The smell of such cobras is muted, tainted by their limited lives of burlap existence. But, mixed with residual smell of fakir's fear (for he never truly knows or trusts his cobra), it is still a thought-severing smell. What it will provoke is never certain. Sometimes it is a nervous laughter. Sometimes it is an almost unbearable silence. And this is true of man, of woman, and of child. For whatever their private thoughts and passions, they are rapt by this ceremony. And they know its rules. It must truly be cobra and it must truly have fangs and poison. The fakir must sit within the deadly arc of its strike and endure a span of time therein, mingling his body with the cobra's aura. What secret pact may exist between them, if any, is never revealed. Perhaps, when the crowd has dispersed, he quickly pops a fat mouse in the cobra's basket, thinking, "Now, my lovely, you will spare me another day, even though I should probably survive your sharp kiss." But in fact he does not know. He never knows. At the heart of cobra is always uncertainty, mystery, and betrayal. For cobra lives elsewhere. And the crowd knows this, too, muted as the ceremony is. There is always that edge of expectation that is esthetic and even spiritual. Cobra may strike, and fakir, though he may live, will writhe and groan, and all those around him will be transported into an awful ecstasy that will linger drunkenly in their minds for days.

Now I say all this, by the way, because I am thinking of getting married to a truly wonderful woman of many and varied talents. But before I get to her, for this is really her story, I have a few more details about cobra that I must recount. I might as well be complete. The raw encounter in the forest with cobra is, as I have said, as rare as it is extraordinary. And thus we surmise about that experience, phantasmagorize. But there is one realm where the encounter has been toyed with beyond our actual knowledge, and that is in films of a certain order. I put it that way because it would be wrong to say simply that they are bad films. That is true: they are bad films by classic or modern standards. They lack a certain rigor or robustness of reality. But that is irrelevant. For within their badness, within their mewling conventions, something lurks. There is, for example, a true representation of the fakir's crowd, the numbing exhilaration reflected in their eyes as their breathing escapes their control, and the deep musk miasma of cobra (which actually wafts through theater). There are many variations of the representation, but I like best the encounter in the cave, the remote cave so difficult of access. Most often it is a young man, rather like myself, who is called upon to seek the cave, penitently and credulous, a task imposed upon him, a redemption at hand perhaps, and there, kneeling in utter isolation, to call forth the monstrous cobra therein residing. It will approach him, its head swaying slightly above his own, and they stare at each other, inches and eons apart. The young man, who has a plain young woman, his betrothed, waiting for him in the village, praying for his success, must lean forward and kiss the cobra thrice on its body, each time exposing his neck to the deadly downward thrust. The camera focuses in on his sweating face and his terrorized eyes. He knows that at any moment, with a flick of its head, cobra could sting him into oblivion. And, in fact, at times he cannot be sure this has not happened. His vision blurs, he hallucinates, the potent musk smell has obliterated his capacity to breathe freely, he staggers into other realms of being. Sometimes cobra becomes a luscious naked woman, with swelling breasts topped by dark petulant dancing nipples, thrusting dark voluptuous corners of flesh at him. He wants to rush madly forward, to engulf and engorge himself. But he does not, for he never forgets the flicking tongue, the dark eyes, and the cradled fangs. Sometimes the face of this beauty seems to be that of his village betrothed, and she laughs tauntingly. She confuses and frightens him. "Is it you? Is it really you?" he thinks. "Is this what lies beneath your demure sari?" But as he leans nearer to see, the snake hisses and he is immobilized again by profound fear. We eventually do see the first two kisses. But we are already worn with anxiety. We grip our seats. We are in the Indian village, gathered around the fakir, our breaths unruly. How wondrous that such a bad movie can do this to us. A few of us may even laugh at the ridiculousness of it all. But watch it we shall, for we must see the third kiss, the kiss that will mean success or death (and it is understood, of course, that success here is always limited). And of course we never really do see the third kiss, for always, as the young man leans for his desperate final act, the serpent lunges, fangs flashing suddenly with a roar of hiss to meet his kiss. And his blur of vision becomes ours as he collapses in a confrontation too fearful and exalted for his system, or ours, to endure. We next see him regaining consciousness and composure on the cave's floor, alone, alive, apparently successful. He cannot believe his luck, his victory, and scrambles to his feet, looking around nervously. He leaves the cave smiling, possibly even laughing, exultant, and goes crashing through the brush to claim his bride, forgetting all the thick and terrifying aura of the cave and its dweller. Soon it will be a dream, then a legend. Soon he will prance around the village. The rains will come. The crops will be good. Soon he will have children. But for us—cobra is still in its cave. For cobra is immortal. Cobra still awaits. And none of us, none, knows when or why he will be called upon to make that unholy pilgrimage, face that unfathomable presence.

    Now I mention all this because I am, as I say, considering marriage to a wonderful woman—beautiful, a lawyer, healthy, an excellent cook, with wide hips, from a good family, clean, and of marvelous disposition. We have engaged on many levels, including the sexual, with complete compatibility and joy. I am much envied. I have every prospect of leading an exemplary and long life and fathering handsome and intelligent children. Except for one thing. Which is difficult to explain. I think it began (and probably ended) with an innocent but very sincere comment of mine. On one of our mornings-after (a cute phrase she berates me for) I said to her, "Women have a difficult time in America." Now my fiancée is what is called a liberal and a feminist. She uses the word epistemology correctly. She is not uninfluenced by the many grave women who have spoken on the lot of women in the world. So she sat up and, as they say, took notice. She was pleased. If she was puzzled by my timing (as I, subsequently, was) she did not say so. The statement obviously deepened our already satisfactory relationship. She was ready for me to say more, to expand on the subject. I had, after all, merely made an introductory remark. But in fact I didn't have anything more to say. The phrase had, for some unaccountable reason, popped into my head. Aware of her expectation, I became anxious to formulate some chapter and verse, some suitable statute, for her. She prodded me by asking, finally, "What, exactly, do you mean?" Now that "exactly" is my fiancée in a nutshell. She loves to cross her t's and dot her i's. What I *mean* is not enough: it has to be what I mean, *exactly*. If anywhere, it is here (or there) that we have a dividing of paths. I have a lamentable tendency toward murk, which I struggle against and about which she jokes. I have problems with language, for example. Simple words will suddenly seem quite mysterious to me and I am almost afraid to use them. So I mumble and stutter and seem unable even to tell the time or give simple direction at times. She in contrast is strikingly clear, like a cold pellucid pool. Her intelligence awes me. She is never at a loss for words or solutions, whereas I am just the opposite. I am at a loss for everything. I admire her strength and confidence enormously. I suppose I am somewhat intimidated, too. Her mere presence trivializes me, or so I think at odd moments, wondering why I was not born a raccoon or beaver or some other creature more commensurate with my talents. But this digresses. What did I answer her? What did I say? "Well," I said, "have you noticed, for example, how many women look like bag ladies? I mean, in one way or another. On the same continuum." I knew the moment I spoke that I was in deep trouble. (It is no relief to note that for me uttering words is always a form of deep trouble.) Her face, her body, perceptibly hardened. I was going to be held to a very strict account for my words. And yet, how could I explain myself? How could I tell her that no such thing is possible? Would she believe that my words, such as they were, stemmed from the greatest sympathy for the plight of women? If it came to that, could I believe it myself? I was grateful that I had not actually articulated the word plight. I should have been immediately finished with that. My mind, giddy with fear, raced. Nothing quaint about bags, purses, or pocketbooks. No Freudianizing or symbolizing over intricate and mysterious interiors. ("And what about wallets?" she would counter. "Tell me about wallets." No, I was quite pinned, encircled, trapped. We knew what I was talking about—that image of the overdressed, shabby, lone, silent figure with her many bags of seemingly useless materials, sitting on the edge of our eyesight, enduring in the same time and space but not a part of anything. When provoked, she might mumble or rave. No one knew where she relieved herself. One rarely saw her eat. Her itineraries and schedules were beyond mystery. Her bags provoked fantasy. The body hidden beneath so many layers of clothing was rarely if ever bathed, and certainly not visualized. She was impervious to touch, sound, family, community, meaning, progress, the weather, the world. Where was she? What was she? And how did she get there?—That woman, give or take a few details, was my bag lady. Now I have since thought about it, and what I meant by my remark was that America is not a place where women, particularly women like my fiancée, *belong*. Men joke about them. No matter what their achievement, the base metal of their social being is their use as object, particularly sexual object. Marriage mitigates and disguises, but only somewhat. Even so, those without a husband feel freakish and incomplete. No matter that they deny this. The merest wisp of a man gives them relief. Even an absent or dead man. And all this, I say, is terrible. It is terrible that in any number of communities in Asia and Africa and Latin America, even in the abjectest servitude, a woman's sense of herself, of her place, of her sex, is infinitely greater than here. Beggars they may have, but no bag ladies. And so what I meant was that all over I see sister bag ladies. They are well-dressed and well-paid, they move with determination, they paint their nails and faces, they smell good, they contribute mightily to the gross national product, they articulate irrefutable cogencies, and so on—but they are still discardable, replaceable, interchangeable. Over a certain age they barely exist. They are two, or five, or ten steps from the bundled figure in the doorway. Because they do not matter, their securities are always the thinnest ice, beneath which they can be frozen out of life and society. Women know this, as well as men. And it gives them unending jitters, a shrillness, a sharpness, anger and hostility that only exacerbates their fundamental unease and sometimes makes them difficult to sleep or cohabit with. But what can they do? Slit their throats? Cut themselves off from men? They feel what is only too visible. They know about the innumerable quiet and unseen bag ladies drooling in old age homes, on benches and in museums everywhere, in drab rooms in drab houses, in drab communities. Indeed, they are related to them. Quite unconsciously they see their fellow vibrant women often as on a fast or slow track to bag ladydom with portfolio, especially if they are over thirty and unmarried. But they cannot, they will not, say it, recognize it, live with it and with the awesome, demoralizing consequences such a confrontation would bring. I think my fiancée was at one point about to ask me whether I thought she was, or was becoming, a bag lady, whether that was indeed what I was saying. But she did not ask. Perhaps it would have cleared the air. Perhaps it would only have ruined life and romance for her, as some questions always do ("Am I desirable?"—Do not hesitate one second!) More and more women should obviously die or disappear at a young age, before such questions loom. If they live or insist on being visible long enough, they will sooner or later be afraid to turn corners for fear of what they will see (what else are they holding at bay in all those reflecting surfaces?).

As you might have guessed, I did not say all this to my fiancée. I thought of it only later, although it must have been in me already. I was too tongue-tied. It was all too complicated. I was not about to rewrite history or get further entangled in language. Or make a speech: rhetoric is a pretty killer. What would she have said—"My god, you don't understand me at all"? Anyway, she must have guessed a lot, for she quite literally reared herself before me. I was aghast at her unspeakable prescience.

There I was bursting with *sympathy* (an ugly, ugly word, I know) for the lot of women and I was scared to death. I should mention that my fiancée—I suppose I should say my former fiancée—although she dresses quite smartly for her profession and wears clicky smart heels, an expensive and subtle scent, on her weekends favors sneakers, multiple socks, and overlapping layers of peasant fabrics, often with a tunic or jumper, the colors and designs thoroughly clashing. It is her act of solidarity with "sisters" everywhere, a defiance of the sources of her large salary. I suppose I might say she is a kind of cute hippy bag lady with clean underwear and pleasant ideologies of love and brotherhood and the preservation of the planet. But what would be the point? Would she understand me? Would she love me? Far better to return to the cave, to cobra, dear deadly cobra. No speech is necessary there, and that awful fulfillment reaches deep inside me. Sometimes the path is through hot lava pools (an odd intrusion from a different but parallel type film, often called the volcano/quest film), where one slip would mean boiling to death. Sometimes there is a jungle, too, but earlier, preceding the lava, thickets with leeches perhaps, dangerous rustlings, savage eyes and unknown fate. But usually the cave is reached, remote, barren sometimes, other times with richly appointed altar and tapestries. It depends, I suppose, on the movie's budget, the director, the supposed audience, whether it is filmed on location or a back lot. But cobra is always there. And no fakir cobra, this, but something primeval, slithering slowly from the cave's labyrinthine recesses, arising to awesome height, tongue flickering, spreading its musk smell so repulsive yet compelling, unwavering black eyes, firm, powerful body, and long, long fangs tucked within, sharper than needle, swifter than light, rooted in repository of ultimate liquid, noxious secretion, I lean, lean, lean forever forward, forward toward life and death's third kiss.

<u>Notes</u>:

These few jottings are here appended because they do not fit the above text smoothly. I claim no specific relevance for them but nevertheless include them for the rare connoisseur who might indulge by them a specialized taste, however incomprehensible to the rest of us.

1. *Cobra's forked tongue.* Misleading in that all snakes have forked tongues. Why focus especially on the cobra? Perhaps because cobra, being so large in size and potent in poison, we see her darting tongue as equally awesome. A little known Iraqi tribe in a vast and remote swamp of their nation has a peculiar and no doubt (to us) barbaric custom regarding their own species of cobra. Several prize specimens are seized each year before the rainy season (a nightmarish downpour) and in a nighttime cere-

mony their tongues are removed. I forebear to mention the gruesome details by which the tongues are removed—they are both savage and dangerous; I will mention only that the ceremony is performed to a chorus of wails and shrieks by the young unmarried women of the tribe as they smear themselves with blood saved from various slaughterings. At high noon the next day the snakes are released into the surrounding morass, and, lacking one of their primary organs of sense, they do many antic things. The villagers mock them and laugh uproariously, and despite the fact that the cobras still have fangs, the villagers jump and roll dangerously close to them in their mucky realm. Occasionally one of them is stung and dies, sometimes by a totally new cobra. By mid-afternoon the snakes are all gone and the young women remain in the village clearing (high ground), unwashed, until the rains come and cleanse them. It is rare that anyone ever finds the carcass of one of these de-tongued cobras after the rainy season, but anyone who does is considered a blessed individual and is thereafter called *He Who Is Master of the Cobra without Tongu*e. In proof of this he hangs the dead cobra on a pole outside his dwelling for all to see.

The human analog to cobra's tongue is much attenuated, possibly spurious. Sometimes the darting in and out of the human tongue is suggestive of gustatory anticipation, as in comedic situations, or sexual intention, again as in comedic situations. More often it is associated with famous vamps of screen, either flagrantly, the organ lavishly displayed and withdrawn, or muted, just the tip protruding coquettishly or licking glistening lips. Imitations among the general populace are invariably ludicrous. Nevertheless, it is well documented in certain psychological texts that not only is there a frequent desire on a partner's part to grasp the other's tongue boldly within his or her mouth but an actual desire (in some few instances carried out) to clamp down upon it with the teeth and savagely rip it out. At those moments, much more than mere tongue has been extirpated, but mind, psyche, and even language are usually unequal to the implications. At best, medical and legal interventions are quickly put in place, and a communal narcosis is the only chorus for the now forever mute young man (or woman). Had they lived in the Iraqi village, they would have been honorably dubbed *He (or She) Who Knows but Cannot Speak*, converse of civilization's honorific, *He (or She) Who Speaks but Cannot Know.*

(We probably grossly misappropriate the American Indian's mythology of the "white" man speaking with forked tongue as a metaphor for lying, I think. If we examine the forked tongue as, say, a metaphor for the possibilities of the famous excluded middle we might shed light not only on the Indian *vis-a-vis* white civilization but on our subject generally: cobra contains both equal and opposite ends in one embodiment, hence a new world of possibility.)

2. *The circus handlers*. There is no difficulty with the zoo handlers of cobra. They merely cater to our unnatural voyeurism (I don't think we dwell enough on our peeping upon the confined of the animal world, a perverse and misguided ethology at best, akin to our perverse anthropologies). However, cobra is not so readily associated with the circus. There one expects the long heavy bodies of pythons, boa constrictors, and anacondas, lovingly intertwined with the near-naked bodies of young women, often as they recline on couches or pillows. This causes goose bumps enough, but it does not approach the dimensions of cobra. It is superficial and crass. It is usually the smaller, more motley, less financed troupes, the carnivals and side-shows, that advertise their cobra horrors (or what they hucksterishly disguise as cobra horrors). They thread our sleazier byways and operate often beneath notice. And it is among the onlookers of these groups that there are assembled something close to the village fakir's audience. Remote as are these revelers from the jungles in which king cobra glides, and as clumsy or transparent as are the exhibitions contrived for them, they nevertheless imbibe an irrefrangible thrill from whatever staging is enacted. And when they return to their farm or

suburban lawn or town tenement, they remain for a while alert to other possibilities in the grasses, in dank cellars, in back yards, shivering at rustlings, movements heard but not seen, odd and new noises. And then they dream. And then they forget. But in another spring or summer they return to view again any fakery with cobra offered, for something in them has been hooked as firmly as any great fish might be, and however long the line, they feel the pull, for cobra is different from the lazy, often drugged, long snakes and young female bodies they are more familiar with, different and far darker, darker and more frightening, as frightening as oblivion.

3. *Smelling cobra.* An understandable enough phrase in itself. Perhaps, on the face of it, an absurdity, an insanity. What it lacks, as I have said, is documentation. How unfortunate that the circus denizen is so illiterate, uncommunicating, and inarticulate. For skulking by cobra's cage by day and sometimes even sleeping by it at night, he lives another existence. He is drawn to the very thing that would kill him if it could, that *will* kill him if he is forgetful or careless just once, for cobra is, in essence, unpredictable. Perhaps he was drawn to his duties from the beginning by some intransigent aroma in his head. Perhaps he is one of those poor souls who has advanced from biting off live chickens' heads in the sawdust to his present station. No matter. All are captured by

cobra's smell, but none may tell, none *can* tell of what they know. Only sometimes by close observation of such, by spying on their furtive inhalations, noting their marvelous tics, so to speak, can one get an inkling of what must be cobra smell. But if one gets that close, one is tempted to go all the way. From that inclination there is often no safe returning. Close observation can easily become secret fraternity, even community—cobra smellers unincorporated, say, or the illuminati of the lair (a term I prefer here to cave).

4. *Lesser breeds.* It has occurred to me that living in the civilized world, I have meager access to cobra-cult, although I am certain that pockets of it exist in its raw state even here. Thus the idea of securing something like a corn or rat snake, even a ribbon-backed garter, has crossed my mind. Lesser poisonous snakes like the pigmy rattler, the bushmaster, or black mamba (how arrogant to speak so lightly of them—but cobra-cultism promotes an eerie arrogance) are illegal but available on the black market, an interesting example of the space between us and the culture of an Indian or African village. I do not feel up to abrogating my cultural context so flagrantly. However, a slim ribbon-back, if I suffused myself with it, might at least put me in striking range of cobra-cult intensities. For example, I have seen *children* familiarly coax these creatures up their sleeves, down their backs, and into pock-

ets. I have something more daring in mind, suggested by various yoga-like practices with string, rope, rough-napped towels, etc. For example, I have read that with proper application one can sever one's tongue sufficiently to swallow and retrieve it at will. I have read also that the great sumo wrestlers of Japan can retract their testes into the body cavity for protection during their bouts, allowing them to descend at their leisure afterwards. What I have in mind is training my ribbon-back to slide up my nostril, past my tonsils to my throat, and thence over my tongue and out my mouth, all the while carefully regulating my breathing and provoking the utmost sense of smell. That might well, I think, put me near the cobra-smeller's ontic moment. I have thought also but not yet researched the feeding of my ribbon-back through my nostril and out my ear. Of course, it is theoretically possible, I suppose, to swallow my ribbon-back whole and have it emerge finally, after many twistings and turnings, at my other end, but living in a society so devoid of internal worms and parasites, I think I would have difficulty in training myself and my ribbon-back to this purpose. Perhaps simply regurgitating it after a period of nestling deep in my throat or even lower would be more practical. And needless to say, all of my exertions in this direction would have to be carefully screened from others, although I dare say something in my demeanor would reveal to the cognoscenti who and what I really was. In this area I confess to one recurring mad impulse—namely to be in the midst of society (at a conference of learned minds, a dinner party, sitting in a library's public reading room, purchasing some new artifact for my home) and to allow, with complete nonchalance, my slim ribbon-back to emerge from my nostril to my mouth, or (who knows?) even from my eyeball and to note its reception. This is an impulse, however, I am reasonably certain I could suppress, however salutary might be its expression for the common weal.

5. *The smell of other peoples*. I have been aware for some time of the smells of other peoples. There is a rankness, an odor of moist and rotted leaves, certain dank earths and wet walls about them that is for me on the same continuum as cobra. Perhaps I am wrong about this. Perhaps instead of smelling sweet or neutral to them I smell equally rank—and I know that I am not on that continuum, even when sick or constipated. Am I being unduly romantic? Is their excrement really more acceptable than mine? I don't know. Even unwashed, I find something lacking about myself. Does my sweet flesh ooze too much progress, too many chemicals, foods too refined? Would my ribbon-back begin to change that? A little of my ex-fiancée's epistemology might, I think, be useful here.

5A. Quite clearly there are musk pheromones wafting beneath the business and the busyness of our orders. Equally clearly their registration is subliminal and their effect undesignated. In effect, cobra, so to speak, slithers in our closets and lurks in our drawers. But even were cobra suddenly to plug our mouths, we would not grant cobra existence. Our streets are filled with people who wear the frozen expression of those whose vital passages have been stoppered. Were pants to be dropped and skirts lifted, many a bottom would reveal the dangling cobra head.

6. All true cities of the world contain labyrinths, and all labyrinths are connected, and lead to cobra's lair.

7. *The cobra's hood.* Unmentioned up to now. Oddly. Yet the most dreaded cobras of all have their hood, that fearsome lateral expansion framing its head, that swollen fleshly flange which invariably means cobra is at full readiness to inflict

> An Ardour 'twere more bless&eacute;d to forego
> Than receive.

The hood has by some been dubbed the cobra's braid or tress, but not by anyone who has been in cobra's aroused proximity. The appellation is absurd. For cobra's hood has little of mere ornament in it. Muscular, pulsating, rock-swollen with viscous fluids, its quivering shape constantly changing, fierce embrasure of deadliness, it very likely empowers the spitting of cobra's venom, the first and kinder blindness of its only drama.

8. The Polynesian volcano-quest parallel usually features a reverse situation to cobra's lair. Instead of cobra we have a male god, often called Tagaloa, who demands the sacrifice of a beautiful and nubile young woman (as in the Kong legend?). And instead of the cave we have the seething lava within the volcanic cone. To allay Tagaloa's anger, she must hurl herself or be hurled into his hot lava mouth. The village or island is thereby saved for a period of time, but the young man in love with the maiden must satisfy himself with a second order female, with appropriate chanting and ceremony, emblematic of the civilizing process. Should he dare to flee with the original maiden, Tagaloa, unappeased, unable to contain himself, would explode and spatter the island with his hot wrath. The major difference seems to be the substitution of a male-dominated for a female-dominated mythology. But in both cases, certain experiences are sacrosanct, on the dim border between man and god. One challenges them only with great risk. And sacrifice is essential. An American parallel may be dimly discerned in the so-called stag party the eve before marriage, wherein the groom is a participant in a drunken debauch that serves as a lamentation of loss rather than a celebration of gain or a ritual of transition or enactment. The woman who bursts

naked from a cake or the strip dancer who welcomes all comers is a far cry from cobra or lava bed. The groom's subsequent (unconsecrated) life is, of course, suitably inscribed by this as well as by the laughable rice-throwing the following morn, occasionally producing low-level pathos.

9. The reason we can never truly see the third kiss is that we either would not believe it, and the entire film would thereby be vitiated, or (if we did truly see it) we should have to die, at least metaphorically, a psychic physic we probably could not endure.

10. The village girl might, in fact, *be* cobra woman. What is needed is to smell her carefully with the eyes closed. Only then might she slowly unfold her fangs.

11. It is said that when the young man enters the cobra's lair he calls her forth. But how? Obviously it is nothing simple or crude like a whistle. There are only three possibilities. If cobra has attendants, seen or unseen, they might initiate the proceedings (by, say, striking a gong). The young man might simply remain silent and humble, knowing that cobra will sense his presence and purpose and will in due time appear. Or the young man might chant or recite some litany, some memorized prayer, words reserved for this occasion alone, cobra appearing to perform her prescribed

role. There might also be rites before the cave such as cleansing, appropriate garb, ceremonial farewell, and so on, without which no calling forth could succeed. Clearly, whatever method is used, everything is all of a piece. It is a seamless journey and quest. Nothing disturbs it.

12. *Cobra's lair.* Who are cobra's attendants? I repeat: *who are cobra's attendants?* From what ranks? With what duties?

13. Finally a word about fiancée. Her name is Helen, but close friends call her Poopsie. I have drawn the line at Poopsie.

# THE MONEY IN MY LIFE

My life and money is a simple story. I am not in this world to make money. I do not object to *having* money, only to working specifically to *make* money. Should money *flow* to me as a consequence of doing something I wish to do, that is satisfactory. Obviously that doesn't happen often. However, since money can be useful, I have several strategies to increase it. For example, I *save* money, in the peasant manner my grandmother taught me. I also periodically invest in a game of chance. So far I have won nothing. Not infrequently, I find money, mostly pennies, on the sidewalk or street, and I almost always pick them up. When do I not? When they look too battered or soiled, as with garbage or spittle, perhaps dog feces, litter, and so on. A minor fantasy of mine is that I will be struck by a truck while bending over to pick up a penny. In the fantasy it is always a truck, and I am always struck from behind. I find that in this, the retrieval of pennies, I am in an increasing minority (interesting phrase). Fewer and fewer people pick up pennies. Or even nickels. To do so is very likely a sign of age. Young people have newer dignities. I used to save my found pennies as a form of good luck until it became too difficult to turn them in at banks in bulk. Banks too have their dignities. Now I spend my luck as I get it, and go to banks only with folding money, I have a slight philosophical problem with picking up pennies. I like to think that I am interested in the world, that I keep alert to the flow of life by me. But more often than I like I find my eyes focused below that horizon. I do not simply *find* pennies. I *look* for them. My eyes are focused downward. And I feel vaguely guilty about this. For example, instead of at people I am looking at refuse, a certain detritus, a truncated humanity. I feel I am abdicating a social obligation, a communality. And, in effect, when I am thus tethered, I *am* working just for the money. There is also a certain peculiarity about it. I have never, for example, seen a bag lady pick up a penny. Indeed, once I picked up a *dime* next to a street beggar and skulked off. What I do is beneath them. I know some people smirk when they see me stoop. Such money is truly dirty for them. What, then, am I? Even when I amass my pennies to buy, say, half a newspaper, they are accepted with a vast indulgence rather than a convenient addition to the vender's small change. It is not clean money. It is cuckoo money. My own children do not pick up pennies and are ashamed when they see me do so. (Of course I restrain myself if they have friends with them.) Immigrants disdain street pennies. They are no way to begin life in America. If I am dressed in my business clothes, so much the worse when I bend. For the educated, I am neurotic, a deviant, possibly dangerous. For many of the newly arrived I am their first quaint experience of a Jew, although I am not Jewish. My wife is tolerant. She remembers hard times and knows me as a decent sort. Although, in fact, I have more than pennies in my life's economic repertoire, it is the pennies that seem to matter most. They are like the particularities of character that are also being shed in the service of some higher economy. I have come, for that reason, to enjoy the company of fools and bores a great deal. Their stunning awkwardness is so much like the penny in the gutter. A few weeks ago, crossing a barrio street (where pennies, oddly, are more frequent than elsewhere), I bent over to scoop a coin and twisted my back because it would not come loose. someone had glued it to the pavement to trap such a one as myself. A fat idler watched and smiled. "No problemo," he said. Then I turned and saw the truck bearing down on me. Would my obituary have said that I died for a principle? I doubt it. Who could know? Who could articulate it? The best thing you can say for my salvaging pennies is that no one is going to kill me in competition for them. Somewhere I think my dead mother and father approve of what I am doing. I feel a link. I sense—dare I say it?—the pull of tradition. But we penny-pickers are nearly a secret society. Occasionally we exchange a haunted but friendly look. We cannot save each other from the trucks or the stampeding crowd, but we would drag each other to the gutter and wait until a vehicle arrived to carry us away. Yet, alienated as I am, I feel I have still further to go in my penny-plucking enterprise. What of the coins even I disdain? Should not even they be collected? Collected with the help of a rag if necessary and later cleaned? Surely, then, even friends would slowly abandon me. Friends? It is really difficult to know friends until you are down to final coins. Horizons are difficult to assess. I like looking into a smiling face as much as anybody. But teeth are beginning to worry me. They are too even, too white. And as I slowly bend over, the smile changes. Then I look at the eyes. "Listen," I want to say, "that little hair under your nose that you didn't clip, I love it." How wonderful that you missed it. That hair is really you." Or to some luscious lady—"Show me your secret fat and we shall love it together!" But the eyes are empty. Is it any wonder the trucks find me? They are mobilized into a secret duty—to flatten me like the pennies. And I fear, I shall not be a very pickable one.

# TRIMMING HEDGE

*"Time is the system that must prevent everything from happening at once."*
         —Cess Nooteboom, *The Following Story*

It has occurred to me, as of course it must have occurred to just about everyone else, that to speak of an appointment at 6:15, or any other time, is a strange declaration. Yet the world is clearly hung in the balance of it, just as punctuality confers a virtue of great depth and no meaning. I should be accounted a madman were I to announce that henceforth days should be confirmed by the floating of a balloon of a particular color and that days should not occur in their absence. "But how, sir, will you tell when the slaughter of such and such took place?" some fellow will ask. "Ah," I will slyly smile, "but did it take place at all?" Then will come the congregation of the scratching heads. "Come, come, a joke is a joke, but this is idiocy." And if on such an occasion I should depart with the prettiest girl of all, their impatience with me will turn to rage. What depredations might I be making upon her navel, what dimple will I profane? And she, she, will she be laughing, finding not the least thing wrong, nothing awry, no dark cloud in the sky? Such madmen must, at the very least, be killed so other men may sleep.

    Of course I should like the manner and moment of my killing to be noted in some way. In this, at least, I am a community person. I have vanity. I would wish to belong to inglorious history. But the shadow of irony, the self-mocking laugh, would remain. "Do you really wish a date, sir? Do you wish an actual report on the news?" Well, perhaps not, after all. The fact is, my death and its manner cannot be told, so multitudinous would it be. And there again I am becoming disconcerting. But am I more ridiculous than my neighbor, who declared that the people's justice is never mistaken, or the croaking of frogs? I think not. My neighbor has no nightmares and keeps his lawn trim. Of course, he issues no orders of transport or execution. He is in fact a secret capitalist. But for him, just as every second of the clock is sound, so too is he content to designate crimes and punishments. His scale of worthiness and unworthiness is absolute. Just the other day I helped him trim his hedge. Of course he thanked me. He has friends coming to visit and wanted his domain to look just so. But when I said, "Don't mention it," he looked disturbed. He has had dealings with me before. "Of course I should mention it," he said. "I owe you one." "You've always owed me one," I said. "That's the way it is." He began to sputter, so I quickly suggested he could help me paint my house if he wished. He turned pale. "Or I could help you paint yours," I added. "It's all really so much bigger. I don't have any book for it." All our conversations seemed to go that way. My references dissolve long before the mid-distance. Given the right circumstances, I know he could have me shot. And that bothers me. Does it bother him? I don't know. I do know that it bothers him when I do not support good causes. How can I not support good causes? In some mysterious way, he thinks, I must be opposed to good causes. But that is not so. I do not support *his* good causes because the manner of his good causes can kill.

    His wife is another matter. Occasionally she wonders how she ever got tied up with him. But she has been convinced that his good causes must be supported and that she is virtuous as a consequence. Secretly, I am convinced, she hates his good causes. I say this because we joke together a lot. We talk nonsense, always a good sign. If the people's justice condemned me, she would weep. But she has two children and is twelve years into his system. One day, I asked her, "What do you really think of Charley?" "Oh, Charley," she said, and suddenly cried. No one had ever thought to ask her this important question. "You are a very beautiful woman," I said, and she cried all the more. She would have no problem helping me paint my house in return for trimming her hedge. In fact, if I told her Tuesday was really Wednesday she would not mind at all and would even adjust her life to that fact.

She would not live any less. Charley, however, would probably divorce her and get custody of the children. In his scheme of things, she would have become an unworthy person. She would be up against the wall, with me.

What puzzles me, but not too much, is why Charley accepts my offer to help him trim his hedge. The fact is that Charley has his hedge trimmed in many ways, and I take a nasty pleasure in being a part of it. I like smelling him rot inside. But I also know Charley is a winner. He will bide his time and then, one day, when the situation is ripe, he will say, "Let me help you prune your pear tree." He isn't going to be dragged into anything by me. Of course, I will accept, even though it is a little like having the noose tightened around your neck. In a good cause.

# THE QUEEN OF MOTHS

It is possible that I have become the slave of my fantasies. Last night: hot. The insects: incredibly bothersome. Particularly the moths. For weeks I have been watching them before I put out the light, waiting like a spider for them to hit my flypaper, watching them flutter desperately, listening to them drone, occasionally being impressed by some few that escape by crawling upon the bodies of their brothers. Sometimes they escape only to drop with a crack or a plop and die, buzzing, from exhaustion. Or they fly off with enough stickiness to cause them to struggle wherever they land. What can be the nature of their frustration then? Usually, once I put out the light their activity diminishes and I sleep without difficulty. But last night the heat brought them to some mysterious peak of expenditure, and in the dark they buzzed into my exposed parts and crawled under the cover onto my unexposed parts. I slashed my arms about, sometimes frantically, I confess, but they kept coming. Finally, not to waste the time, I put the light on, read until groggy, and tried again to sleep. It was no good. I lay there awake, sweating, and much bothered. It was then, in that mini-state of torture, that I had my thought: *do moths bite?* And almost immediately: of course not. But they do have mouths, and things do go into their mouths, their mouths do close over things. Why not human flesh, too? Perhaps, of course, they do, but we cannot feel it. In which case, why? and how interesting. From moths my mind moved on to other creatures which might bite but do not, or do so without effect. For example, frogs (and toads). Such a big mouth. Teeth? Probably not. Just a long flickering scroll of a tongue. But nevertheless a mouth. What would it be like to feel those filmy gums on, say, one's finger? Mother, I've been bitten by a frog but you can't see it. (*It... What?*) Why such a big mouth if only small insects go into it? A frog *should* have teeth. And bees. Bees, of course, sting. But there is, in addition to their stinger, a mouth. Who has been bitten by a bee's mouth? (*There* is a distinguished person.) I mentioned these ruminations to my wife (who slept quite well) and she said they were fantasies of sexual fear. The frog (and the moth and the bee) were symbols of the female genital. She got quite elaborate, speaking about the fur of moths and bees, the croaking of frogs, swamps and hives, and nectar, stingers, and several things which I have managed to forget. She has not been much help. Was she teasing me? Or even, perhaps, being *cruel*? And then, the central image of her offhand comments, what am I to make of that? That is, if my wife's sexual part is a frog (or a moth or bee—does a *snail* have teeth?), *what is my wife?* She has, in fact, raised many more questions than she has answered. An extreme question is this one: would there really be anything wrong with thinking my wife's sexual part was a frog's mouth? Or a moth's? Or a bee's? (She would no doubt answer, why bother with her when there are so many frogs in the pond?) Another question: is it possible that *she* feels she has a frog between her legs, and if so what am I?) There is ultimately, of course, the question of where the moths really come from. I do, after all, have *screens* on my windows. I never see them during the day. And they do not, apparently, bother *her*. It is August now, and I have weeks left before cooler weather. I know the fireflies peak in mid-August and then disappear rapidly. I do not know about moths. I look forward to the snow and ice, but there are questions about eggs and woolen things I want answered. But I shall not ask my wife about them because she clearly has her own ideas. And I am beginning to wonder about them.

Notes:

1. Does the activity of moths really diminish when the light goes out? Or do I, in falling asleep, fail to take note of them? (Is there possibly *another* answer?)

2. What strange terms, "exposed and unexposed parts." Unexposed: the genitals, buttocks, navel, breasts, nipples, armpits—a sexual ramble. But *back*? *chest*? *shoulders*? Or an exposed *earlobe*? The tongue, I suppose, is an unex-

posed part. And certainly things like the liver and the pituitary. The adenoids: exposed by indirection. Baboons expose their anuses quite gratuitously. And a pretty purple they often are. My love is a purple anus. Civilization is grand. Etc.

3. On the largeness of a frog's mouth: if it had teeth it could eat potatoes.

4. If "female" were pronounced like "tamale" we could have a near rhyme: *female genitale.*

5. Storks, herons, egrets, etc., aspiration to.

6. Snow and ice. I feel there ought to be a question about that. Or an answer.

## FOR IRVING: A CONVERSION

Irving was the most charming fellow you would want to meet. I mean that. At first, of course, you stiffened. Irving did that to people. He was an albuminoid. He was one with Karloff and Chaney, one of the greats. But you soon softened. Because Irving was really a sweet person. He talked just above a whisper in a curiously melodious, high-pitched, singsong voice. And with utmost sincerity. When Irving spoke, you felt like a chosen creature, and although you knew he was brilliant you never felt stupid with him. Another thing, he was nearly blind. His long, cartilaginous nose supported twin microscopes, through which he seemed always to be peering. But never really at this world. That is my most lasting impression of Irving, a sepulchral peering figure. He was ubiquitous in that guise. Once I saw him walking through an IRT subway train and worried lest he fall between the cars and be crushed. Another time I saw him close by a lamppost in Greenwich Village, as if for safety or security. I shouted at him, partly because of a peculiar joy and partly because I knew he would not see me going by. He peered at me in confusion until I identified myself. Then we swapped a few quick reminiscences about school, where we had been, briefly, colleagues. He asked timidly if I thought he might drop by and pay his salutations to the department. I hesitated, because Irving had left under something of a cloud, and then said of course. When I walked on, he was joined by a female, who took him by the arm. She was not a beauty, but neither was she weird. I felt almost like crying at the thought that Irving might be sleeping with her, partaking of *some* of the pleasures of this world. He was so repulsive physically. I have barely gone into it. He had no figure to speak of (he was a wraith) and what he had was bent over. He walked as if a plumb line hung from his nose. His hair was all kinky white although he was only about thirty. But you did not really think of Irving in terms of years. He existed outside of chronology. The ravages in his sad narrow face either reflected all the plagues of history or nothing. And who can understand such woe? He was a kind of emaciated Jewish Uncas. Yet his pale eyes were kind. There was no bitterness in them. No matter what you said, they looked down at you with wonderful sympathy. You felt so human when you talked to Irving. I guess because you pitied him and were happy to give him something to respond to. Irving was well liked by the staff. His brilliance irritated no one. He was writing a dissertation on a mid-European Marxist few of us had even heard of, let alone read. It seemed proper that Irving should be esoteric. But I don't mean to give too strongly the impression that Irving was unearthly. He was also very human. For example, he had an older sister in Williamsburg who was having trouble getting married and who supported his old and sick parents. These were the remnants of his family. They lived more or less in severe poverty from what I could gather. I never questioned Irving too far, though I admit to strong curiosity about them. Irving lived with them also, but since many schools were reluctant to hire him he gave little to the family funds. He helped in other ways. For example, he ate around as much as he could. Faculty cocktail parties were a boon to him; he hovered over the hors d'oeuvre table like some hebephrenic holy spirit. And when we went to a restaurant, Irving was never hungry. But he ate the free pickles and coleslaw, and the extra rolls. If anyone was not as hungry as he thought, Irving "nibbled" from his dish. Similarly, he obtained the books he needed with a minimum of expense. And here he revealed no little sense of humor. For several weeks during our association, Irving teased me regularly with a small piece of yellow paper. It was very old and wrinkled and might well have come from a cave in the Negev. He would glide by my desk with a sly chuckle and, as I looked up, quickly hide the yellow paper. Questions were of no avail. Irving was determined to keep me dangling in suspense. I guessed it had something to do with books because I had been joking with him about the large number of desk copies he had been getting. A large part of his chuckling I was convinced was gloating. We enjoyed the game for several weeks and then very late one Friday afternoon when we were alone in the shadows, he waved the yellow paper in front of my eyes and at last explained the mystery. I could not read the writing. It was, he said, a list publishers. I must have looked astonished because he cackled with great pleasure. They were, he said, the names of publishers from whom he wanted books. I asked him why he didn't put down the names of the books too. Wasn't it difficult to remember which books went with which publisher? I think Irving must have loved me for that question. He let out another loud cackle of glee and showed me all his teeth. It gave me an extraordinary feeling. His laughter was followed by a prolonged "Ahhhh!" as he rolled up the text and put it away carefully. No. That would have been too incriminating. There were forces in this world which he, Irving, must beware of. This way only he knew everything. It turned out to be quite a bit more elaborate. Irving had various academic friends (never named) scattered all over the city. These he freely impersonated on the telephone and ordered desk copies of books in anthropology, history, philosophy, and God knows what else. And only in hard covers. Paper books were not worth the effort. His library must have been immense, stretching from the dawn of man's consciousness to the distant darkness. Apparently Irving's disciples did not mind being his instruments. Perhaps they felt themselves in the service of some higher good which only Irving knew. I suppose a lot of Irving's ubiquitous quality was because of his making the rounds to pick up his treasures. Irving went *everywhere*. The truth of his perigrinations shocked me of course, though I did not let him know. He had really gone too far. But then I said why not. Why shouldn't Irving brighten his dismal existence with something he loved? It was all a rat race anyway, wasn't it? And the publishers could certainly spare the books. At least Irving would read them, and understand them, and keep them from unclean hands. Months after Irving had left, there were rumors about certain books in our own library. But I never credited them. Irving would never have done anything to *us*. And if he had he would have taken only books that were rarely, if ever, read, so that their absence would not be noticed until he was in his grave. Time would have enveloped the deep motives in Irving's life; we should have had only a mystery to mull on. It was shortly after the revelation of the yellow paper that Irving borrowed his first dollar from me. It seemed, at the same time, a strange kind of test of my sincerity. He had had no lunch, he said, and would not be home until late. That exchange was the first of many. I could not have kept track if I had wanted to, for Irving paid my dollars back at odd moments and in odd proportions. Also he overlapped his borrowing and repaying. He had his own unique system of credits and debits, which finally transcended the mere exchange of money, made it, in fact, seem coarse and crude even to attempt exact figures. I have never for a moment worried about the final tally of our economic relationship; in fact, I *miss* giving Irving dollars. He had that quality which made you feel good when you lent him money. You hoped he would forget it. It was all you could do not to offer him more. For the same reason I enjoyed watching him eat. It was as if I said to myself, "Eat, Irving, eat. You, too, deserve to live." I am aware of, and ashamed of, the horrible condescension in what I am saying. But I cannot help it; it is the truth. I think I could have fed Irving myself, it was such a miracle to see him continuing the struggle for life. And he was so grateful. If you said good morning to him, his response was such that you felt like Christ blessing the lepers. You were only too happy to do anything you could for Irving. For example, his fears. Irving had collected them for centuries. If you mentioned casually to him that *they* were after him, it was as if a wind from the tomb had struck him. You quickly retracted, but it did no good. For days, for weeks, he was after you at odd moments, sometimes trying unsuccessfully to joke about it, sometimes wheedling a little. Was it true? Were there rumors about him? What had I heard? Surely some truth lurked even behind my joke, if that was what it was. God knows what harmless crimes lie harbored in his fragile chest. It would have been funny except that he so visibly suffered, actually began to die before your eyes. No man was ever so hounded. It took him several months of Talmudic dialogue with me to decide when to see the chairman about a renewal of his contract. If it was too early wouldn't it be presumptuous? or foolish? But exactly when would it be too late? Should he wait for him to take the first step? What constituted a first step? Perhaps it had already been taken and he had missed it? When was he *least* busy? Should he write? Would it be an insult? What kind of paper, style, heading? Or should he just broach the subject in the flesh? Casually, perhaps, at lunch? No. Never while eating. Did I know what he thought about him? No, of course I couldn't betray any confidences, but… It turned out that it was all for nothing. Unfortunately Irving was not to remain with us. It would have required that all history be rewritten. He was lamentably absent-minded. He was brilliant and made up brilliant examinations. No one in the whole department could have passed. Some of his students broke down in tears when they read his midterms and finals. And I know some students' lives have been permanently touched by Irving's disquisitions on Job. But Irving created chaos. He carried night with him. He never handed in his freshman theme folders until physically threatened. The unfortunate colleague assigned to the task still does not know whether to laugh or cry about his joke. Irving succumbed entirely. He went under. Not that this was all. Whole classes of chattering students periodically stamped into the office for appointments with Irving, but Irving was usually elsewhere, on his way to Spuyten Duyvil, where

Dutchmen once bowled on the green, crossing Washington Square, bound for an obscure shop on East Canal Street—in search of what? That is the thing about Irving. A sepulchral peering figure. He seemed to commune with a world we at best only suspect, certainly never believe, and sometimes, rarely and without knowing, touch. It's a ridiculous statement, but there it is. I believe it. I should never be surprised to see Irving anywhere, and I am often aware that I am looking for Irving as I travel around the city, expecting, even wanting, him suddenly to appear. At first I saw him often. He haunted me. Now it has been more than five years. Recently I thought I'd get a dog, but I gave up the idea. I suddenly felt a terrible emptiness in me. I knew that one night while I was walking it, Irving would appear like a specter. And I would be inadequate to the moment. Sometimes I have dim visions of Irving—Irving amorous (what does he whisper?), Irving the victim of anti-Semites (utterly blind without his glasses!). Sometimes I think Irving could not have been real. He was so ugly, so frail, the most charming fellow you would want to meet. Foolishly, I feel a little less human since Irving went away. But I don't really know what I would say should I meet him. I suspect now I would go right by. He'd never see me. Isn't that the way it is?

## THE MAN WITH BEAST IN HIM

I once knew a man with a wild beast in him. He knew about it, and sometimes close friends joked about his "wild bull of the pampas." He did not fool us with his relative demonstration of the beast. In his own thoughts what raged in him was far more dangerous than a bull. His beast was phantasmagoric. And very occasionally its eyes and his looked out at us simultaneously. His problem was twofold. On the one hand, he feared the beast and was constantly pacifying himself to prevent any eruption. For this reason he bored most people, including his wife, whom he loved dearly. On the other hand, he recognized that he and the beast were, after all, one and that he could not in any real sense *live* unless he liberated him. All his creative energies were bound up in his beast. But although he feared the unbidden manifestation of his beast, he had found no way to make him appear at his command to work miracles for him. So both he and his beast paced restlessly through life, on intimate terms, but neither one a help to the other. His life was decorous and urbane, he was successful enough, he passed through life's essential functions. But underneath it all he smoldered. His beast, growing older and thinner, stormed at all the outposts demanding entry. Only once did it succeed. His wife had understandably been less than satisfied with him. She had early in their marriage sensed an aloofness, a remoteness, an estrangement. She knew, as people who share a bed usually do, that some vital confidence was missing, some commitment or surrender. but being well taken care of and treated with the utmost civility she never broached the subject directly. Instead, in many small ways, she needled him. He was not unaware of the source of her prickliness, but chose to ride it out as being safest for all. Which was a mistake, for she then got no satisfaction at all and became gradually worse. The inevitable result was that one night, weak from a recent illness and lack of sleep, he let the beast out. The beast suited its actions to the occasion. Moaning almost as if it were being slaughtered, the beast feasted in pristine hunger on her body. The love he made to her, his wife, was gross and painful, a love that corresponded only to her dreams and fantasies. It is true that she was responsive, but in being so she became as unfamiliar to herself as was he, and it seemed, when it was over, an indignity she was too old and too settled to bear. The next day, without a word, she left him. He appeared more amused by the whole thing than distraught. His beast, firmly enclosed again, had worked a terrible wreck on his life. How clever of it, he thought, how infernally clever. But if he laughed, however quietly, it would not be wrong to take his laughter as something very different. For he had loved the woman with all his consciousness and hated his inability to be close to her as a lover should. He had tried to compensate with infinite grace, but he had failed. He pieced together his life reasonably well after that, dining with his children occasionally, seeing to it that his wife was well provided for. Once, not long after their separation, she wrote him a letter, vague and rambling, but the thrust of it was clear enough: could some way be found for them to forget that night and to live together once again, perhaps with more understanding? He never answered. Instead, over a period of ten years, he died. I was privileged to be present at his final moments. He said very little, but he looked happy. He was going to emancipate his beast at last. He would crack himself open and let it burst free. I believe he felt on the verge of a new life, and he was actually laughing softly when he died. I would never have noticed but for the cracking sound that interrupted his laughter. Suddenly his eyes were glazed and still. The breath went out of him—or the wind from his emaciated, bleeding bull as it rushed pathetically to gorge and probably choke on ripe fields of green. For just a moment I saw it, I thought, disfiguring him as it squeezed out. And then I was alone with the dead, feeling loss and, inexplicably, fear. I turned, I looked down at my friend of thirty years, *and I saw the beast grinning up at me.* He had come from all the old paintings of nightmare, and his eyes burned into mine with a knowledge I could not face. I turned and went to the nearby window. And there, gazing out at a landscape that yet held back the frost, I wept the first true tears in my life since I was a child.

## EYES, EARS, NOSES

Do you know the sounds of people dying? I don't mean the grand gestures of movies or imagination, the gasps and the aaahs. I mean the little sounds, the syncopated breathing that is more of the dead than the living, the noises of trapped saliva, the hisses of lungs that cannot expand beyond a certain point of pain. They are infinite, these sounds, but only an unencumbered ear can hear them. We have been made dull in our hearing. Perhaps that is why we cannot wiggle our ears any longer. If we could hear, our ears would be *alive* with movement, filtering a thousand sounds of life and death. The same is true of our noses. We have ceased to smell reality, the smells of love, of joy, of fear, of death. For example, sweat alone can reveal any of these qualities to us. Put them together, combine them with our eyes (particularly to see others' eyes), and there is a formidable apparatus for receiving life. I myself have been unbearably lucky in these respects. I was born with the gift to perceive, and I have kept my gift pure. My wife, for example, she is dying. She does not know it yet. No doctor has told her anything. She might last a good many years. But she is dying. I *perceive* it. Her breathing is subtly off. She has smells that sometimes completely turn off my desire to make love to her, particularly in the morning, when her body exudes her most natural smells, uncontaminated by the activities of the day and amenities of civilization. One does not usually want to make love to a moribund thing. And she senses my knowledge, she sees it particularly in my eyes, though she would never admit it to herself. Sometimes I cannot bear the knowing and the waiting. It would be too cruel to tell her. And my son, he lives in abject fear. The essence of him is fear. He quivers continuously, but so imperceptibly that no one can see it. He will wear himself out with his fear and live in a closet, his heart ready to burst. I feel sympathy for him and try to help him. I joke loudly with him, laugh a lot, and slap him on the back. But all that only increases his fear. Every time he sees me it is as if I had leapt out of a box. He looks on the verge of collapse. Of course, sometimes it is too much, it irritates me. Sometimes when I see him and his mother cowering in each other's arms I feel like yelling at them, "Oh, die, you weaklings!" But I forebear. I am very conscious of my good fortune, my superior sense. I cultivate patience and compassion. My friends and acquaintances are also aware of my superiority. That is why they shun me. They are afraid. I am a mirror to their unrecognized, unspoken anxieties. In me they see the unseeable. But how ridiculous. How petty. Would we not all be better off with the truth? Should we not all live with courage? After all, there is joy, too. Is that not compensation enough? I make it a point each day to walk in the midst of nature. There I find no dishonest fear, there is no sniveling. *There* is truth and life and death and beauty. I breathe in, I smell the flowers and the grass and the trees. I feel the wind and the sun. I see the infinity of color. What a joy it all is. How I would like to strip my son naked and have him run there. Poor, timid creature, he would probably die. Perhaps it would be for the best.

# REPRIEVE

I once took in a girl who was close to insanity. I was annoyed that she had chosen me for a refuge, and I tried to get out of it. I explained to her that although I liked her as a person I did not find her attractive sexually. It was no barrier. She was desperate, and moved in at once. Within three nights we had slept together, and continued to do so. I maintained the fiction that she did not attract me, that she was merely a useful body for the purpose of exorcising my lusts. It was a conceit that pleased me; it also left me free. I had the best of playthings, and I owed it nothing. On the other hand, she was greatly in my debt. Not only had I put a roof over her head, but I was, by my presence alone, a barrier to the chaos within her. I did not question her about that chaos. It would have complicated our arrangement, reduced my freedom, given her false hopes. But I could not but perceive something of its nature. The insanity she was holding off was not that kind wherein one has a strong sense of self, albeit perverse. That insanity is often productive and even challenges the conventional categories of sane and insane. No. Her insanity was of the kind that has within it everything, but with no order, no focus, and therefore nothing. The self is obliterated by a whirlwind of people, things, and events. Life is an expanding scream. Nothing but unconsciousness can make it stop, or being plucked out of it bodily and told to do this and do that. This latter is not a solution; it is a reprieve. It is, of course, possible from within this shelter to build pathways out. But it is a slow, tedious business and requires love or money. Unfortunately, she had no money, and I had no love. But I was willing enough to continue to provide shelter, for it simplified my life. It all seemed to me a quite suitable quid quo pro. I pursued my work unfettered. She cleaned, cooked, did odd chores, and slept with me. Occasionally we went out together, to a movie or visiting. She remained totally within my orbit, slept easily, and even sang sometimes. Once or twice I caught a look of absolute terror on her face, as if she realized that nothing but a door stood between her and disintegration. But she always covered up quickly, not wanting to burden me further or disturb me. She had a realistic understanding of her situation. I suppose our friends had such an understanding also, for they never said anything. When we visited, it was obvious that I kept her as an object apart. I took her with me as one might walk someone else's dog, and I counted it a charity. Which is why, I suppose, I became so furious with her. On one occasion, quite out of the blue, she began to speak of me as if we had a relationship. She went so far, even, as to speak jokingly about me as a sex partner. I contained myself sufficiently to manage some diversionary chitchat and an inconspicuous departure. In the street I was silent. There could be no words for my absolute rage and indignation. Back at our rooms I took out my largest suitcase and packed all her things in it. She watched in silence and in tears. I gave her money and led her out the door. I told myself it was the end. But it was not. My rage continued unabated. I could do no work. I felt a great need to destroy. In the end I cried from the frustration of it all. And I slept, quite well. I never saw her again. In fact, no one ever saw her again. She took a room in a hotel and slit her throat, so I was told. I have since received my suitcase back, but have not opened it. My friends appear to pity me. I laugh at them, for I am working better than ever. I have turned my rage into work. I have decided never again to take in a woman. They are too demanding, and in the end always complicate one's life.

# ANTECEDENTS

Some day I should like to make out a case for the antecedentless pronoun. There is a terrorizing grammarian in me, but I have impulses to rebel. For example, when someone says to me, "Isn't it a beautiful day?" the "it" rives me like Ahab's white whale, and I should like to answer, "Yes, but they are after me." And when asked, "Who is after you?" I will say, "Indeed, who is," and laugh. Of course that way lies madness. So I do not act on these impulses. The drama is private. Yet I like to think there might be a residue in my eye, a visible mote that unsettles. For somewhere beneath grammar I am dancing with lunacy, punching holes in my pasteboard mask of contentment. How much longer can I contain it? *It*? Indeed, *it*. The other day a colleague was discoursing on the complex beauty of trees. I knew what he was getting at. "Yes," I replied, "but how much more complex they would be if they were not called trees." He looked at me oddly, finally said, "But what would they be if not trees?" "Something else," I replied. "Everything would be something else." And I laughed rather gleefully. I think I spoiled his lunch. For a moment I even felt invisible. The world was nameless and *I* did not exist. I

## The Man in the Stretcher

have come to realize that *I* is really an antecedentless pronoun. Today *I* am cookies and tomorrow *I* may be pure bile. I think, in spite of my control, people are beginning to avoid me. My laugh, for example, is louder, *elementally* louder. Last week I said to my wife, "Do you realize that you are I? The table is I? Yesterday is I?" She looked at me queerly. (What would we do without queer looks?) I know what she was thinking. That she slept with me. That I was the father of her children. That she had become middle-aged in my company. I meant no harm. "Listen," I said, "look at it this way —" And then, again, I laughed, hysterically. The "it" was too much for me. Of course I could not tell her that. *That*? So I put on my wily joking look, the magician of the universe look. I don't think it worked. When we were younger and I committed some faux pas, I would use that look to squirm out from under. Under *what*? *Where*? Why *squirm*? She would laugh and think me a rascal of some sort. Romance always needs help. But time has dimmed her view of me even as her gaze has become more penetrating. She knows something strange is going on in my head. My children are also aware of something. But it does not bother them yet. They treat me rather like a puppy and often we are a happy if unruly gang. One of the problems from all this (*this*?) is that I don't feel very adult or mature. Somehow I am beyond *them*— those qualities and qualifications. But beyond them *where*? That seems to be my frequent question. Where is my advocacy of antecedentlessness placing me? Clearly grammar requires that pronouns have antecedents. Equally clearly (to me), all such pronouns are a form of butchery. Of course, even the antecedent is a form of butchery. An afternoon of love? Ridiculous. *It*? More ridiculous. I can see that participation in society requires all such butchery. No justice, no love, no truth without violence, why, then, my mad impulses to slip the leash? The awareness of the leash? Do I feel like some metaphysical dog? I have taken to stacking blocks and then knocking them over. I have never until now understood the wonderful anarchy of children. We praise them for the conquest of chaos, their formulations of coherence and order, and then, when they smash them to bits, we are appalled. They, of course, nasty creatures, laugh. What wisdom they lose when they become doctors, lawyers, and Indian chiefs. My wife does not have this affliction. She has too many loads of laundry, the shopping, the cooking, the cleaning, the children. She sticks to her work through thick and thin. My distractions, however, are in one lump—my job. And that (*that*?) is routine. My mind easily floats free. I have decided that my campaign (my *compulsion*) must be disguised and promoted only in stages. I do not wish to be irresponsible, whatever that is, nor to abdicate a position in real life. (Oh, what an antecedent is that!). My children will soon cease to be my playmates, and I do not wish to alienate them or my wife. I have therefore begun to list some actions that will begin to satisfy my interest and not challenge theirs. For example:

1. On occasion, eat my meal backwards.

2. Once a week wear unmatched socks. (A practicality also)

3. Spend one day a week using no pronouns. (It is becoming clearer to me that no pronouns have true antecedents. The distance between them is, at *the* very least, like the distance of time, or space.

4. Spend at least one day a month in total silence, as a tribute to communication and truth.

5. Develop an enigmatic smile as a response to most requests and communications.

6. Cultivate more the company of idiots.

7. Learn one of the remote languages and intersperse it in our table talk and sex life (*Goo tamili tamaka?*).

8. Foreswear the decimal system, etc., e.g., can you give me three socks worth of nuts? Better yet, *your* socks?

9. When discussing family matters like vacation or nights out, be more aimless and indeterminate.

10. Promote long discussions over the meanings of words. What is "garbage" for example, or "whither"? "The."

11. When touring, visit undertakers.

12. Wear leaky rubbers as a constitutional.

13. Change the placement of furniture monthly. Have a furniture-moving party. Enter the house through the window. Have guests and visitors do so.

14. Run the faucet all night.

15. Set traps and give a rat named Plato the run of the house.

These, although fraught with imperfections and peculiar levity obvious to anyone looking (e.g., "monthly"), seem to me mild and good beginnings. They will not disrupt or disturb, but they will, I think, create pockets, maybe crevices, of deeper understanding between my wife and me. As the reader can see, they are almost entirely without domestic perturbations, something to ponder between laundry loads, so to speak. I have not yet ventured into the marketplace, yet should I do so, who knows, I might become rich or famous. The other day I said to my wife, "Have you checked the traps yet today?" "Oh, really?" she answered, and smiled a beautiful asinine smile. Later, I heard her humming and slamming the washing machine lid. I think we can call that progress.

# A PSYCHO-METAPHYSICAL FICTION[1]

I have had two thoughts today,[2] and they seem connected, although I am not sure how. The first has to do with certain professions. Having had dealings with illness and hospitals recently[3] for example, I have been meditating a lot (perhaps even brooding)[4] on doctors. They seem to me entirely worthy of interest, if not wholly admirable creatures. But I do think they are misperceived. They are one of the pinnacles of our society; it is almost unthinkable that anyone could find accession to doctorhood anything less than high achievement, moral and spiritual as well as intellectual. Only lately have their greed and deific posturing come slightly into question, have they been seen as a regulatory agency of cultural and psychic import, and that mostly among

---

[1] I realize this title might seem oxymoronic (or at least evasive), yet it is appropriate. My life seems oxymoronic, too, yet I live it.

[2] I mean, of course, significant thoughts. I try, still, to disengage myself from the irrelevant in life, at the same time retaining a reservation about its potential from another perspective. Which of course gives the show away: everything is relevant, and discrimination amounts to commitment, a moral-political-epistemological stand. So be it: I choose not to be paralyzed, though wrong.

[3] Not that trauma or physical failure are absent from my earlier life. Although I was strenuous in pursuit of sports, I was visited with every childhood illness and several more, the survival from which I owe to my mother's assiduous if sometimes burden-

the cynical, the disgruntled, and the discountable, among whom naturally I number myself.⁵ For most, their standing remains high and pure, and the fact that we (I included) tend to creep to them in weakened and demoralized states, full of mortality and morbidity, reinforces it: a blocked bowel will always preclude criticism or wariness, i.e., we would look kindly even on an ice pick if it promised relief.⁶

However, none of this, as I see it in my pill-dazed mind,* gets to the heart of what is interesting about them (and let us be clear from the beginning that this is a mystery to them as well as

---

some attentions.

⁴ In all senses. I sit upon a foul nest of them, for example. See note #5.

⁵ It seems to me that the natural progression of life is towards disgruntlement and discountability if one focuses on one's humanness. If, however, one focuses on transcendental possibilities, one is sweeter-natured. I am decidedly sour, not having the character to overcome my engorging humanness. As for the "brooding" above, it can be seen as merely one enhatchment of my bile, a bit as if Ahab had focused on a turtle or a duck instead of a whale on the pasteboard mask of life.

⁶ It might seem of some point to declare specifically what I am dying (if I am) from. I prefer not to do so lest it seem that my ruminations be considered merely consequent on ill health or despair, both of which I trade in. Nor should my imagery be taken to heart or lung. *Blockage*, whether of intestine, blood vessel, canal, or nerve pathway, is merely one of several graphic metaphors which are instantly satisfying because instantly understood, as in "ruptured love affair" or "He is a family hemorrhoid." It also has the advantage of economic, psychological, and military application. The most I will say right now is that I suffer from a severe sense of closure, which might or might not be consequent on organic impingements. And this is not to say I would necessarily feel relieved by the reverse, a kind of ongoing diarrhea of life. Yet is there anything in between? (Probably, but it is unnecessary to spell it out).

* The reader, understandably, may already be curious about the writer of this fiction. It is quite natural. To allay anxiety and avoid all element of game, I refer him immediately to endnotes 7, 7A, and 7B, where a certain suitable (formal) embodiment is outlined.

to most of us; this is subcutaneous voyaging). That matter can best be approached by reviewing what it is they actually *do* most of the time. Certainly it is not comforting or consoling, let alone loving, that they do (No doctor ever held my hand); nor is it bookkeeping; it is not even curing (That is almost irrelevant). "Treating" is a curiously more accurate word: doctors "treat" patients. But what is the essence of their "treating?" What *action* are they most often engaged in? What is the physical or metaphysical manifestation of their method? First and foremost, I would say, they *probe*; whether you call it pressing, poking, feeling, pushing, twisting, squeezing, pinching or something else, directly or indirectly, it amounts to probing.[7] However, what they particularly probe are the openings of our bodies: the mouth, the anus, the nose, the urethra, the ears, the vagina. By such openings, through which they seek *entry*, are we hugely known to the medical fraternity. They probe these orifices[8] with their fingers and

---

[7] Probe (selected meanings) n. [ML *proba,* examination, fr. L. *probare,* a slender surgical instrument for examining a cavity; *vt.* to examine with or as if with a probe, to investigate thoroughly; *vi* to make an exploratory investigation. Syn see ENTER.] The "as if," this writer notes, is instructive, as is the use of "cavity" rather than, say, "hole." "[P]robe," of course, is inadequate. A new word is needed; in its absence, "probe" will have to suffice.

[8] My friend the druggist (See endnote 7) has been playful with me over this concern for orifices. I confess the word has a certain resonance for me, containing something official, something religious, something scientific at the same time. Almost the sole remnant of my early days is a passion for the dictionary. And I have meditated more than once on "orifice." I even fantasized once while awaiting an examination that my doctor came out and invited me into his "orifice," on reflection perhaps an unsettling image.

with instruments and liquids. All medications, oral, anal, nasal, vaginal, other, can be seen as a form of probing, as can the insertion of needles into flesh and veins. They probe with their eyes, of course, also (particularly eye to patient's eye, it being orifice to the brain), and no doubt, when they sniff, consciously or unconsciously, with their noses. And when they have exhausted or dismissed these avenues of probing, doctors resort to probing still other cavities of the body, first indirectly through pressure on the unbroken skin, x-rays, and such, and listening devices. Then, often, their sharp edges (slicing, cutting, boring, sawing, chopping) are brought into play, and unnatural orifices, slits in the body, are created, into which, again, the doctors' hands, now contraceptively sheathed, probe among the glistening, sliding organs and voids in the interior of the patient. The needs of medicine, one might say, require the body to exist as endless orifice: the body must be probed for medicine to exercise its darker, truer function. Now, to be sure, it sometimes happens out of all this that pain is relieved, life lengthened, etc., but it is important to understand that this is *incidental*. The essential function is not curing or relieving, but probing. The doctor whose secret and essential as well as public joy is curing and relieving is not a true doctor but something else, perhaps a primitive Christian, or a philanthropist, a philosopher, or even a social reformer or freak.[9] He is a more innocent soul than a true doctor, the prober into our cavities both secret and private (It is no accident that children refer to their genitals as their "privates") for one cannot ignore the violation implicit in the word probe, and therefore the complication of character in those who do it. This is the side of the medical profession we do not see—the doctor as violator of our bodies through probing, then penetrating. There are two things to be said here. First, what is it he seeks? And second, what a strange thing it is for somebody to do, to enjoy, passionately, doing. The answer to the first answers in part the second also. What the prober seeks, of course, is *power*—power through knowledge and mastery of our inner parts. Power is depth; power is penetration. (Doctors of the *surface* of our bodies, mere pimple-poppers, cosmeticians, obviously do not rank as highly as those who probe and penetrate. Similarly, doctors who work with dead or near-dead—elderly—bodies only or solely in laboratories do not partake of the aura of those who probe live, healthy bodies: there is a delicate tension in the probing of a live and healthy body. Women, of course, fecund, naked, and open to master probers, and gynecologists, feel this tension most excruciatingly).[10]

---

[9] It occurs to me that we might easily divide working humanity into two groups, those who practice what they seem to practice and those who do not; and into four subgroups, those with and without awareness of each. As a wholesale dealer in pickles (See endnote7) I have always thought that what I seemed to do was what I in fact did. Now I am not so sure. There is, for example, a peculiar antagonism, not only from my wife (whose chosen name is Olga) but from women in general, that is more than mere dis-

Now, this activity is usually *disguised* as the attempt to relieve pain, serve mankind, etc. But in fact the doctor has little concern with that. His patient is the medium through which he gains power by probing and penetrating. He gladly wears the mask of healer and appears to accept gratitude with grace (He is actually contemptuous of the healed; after all, the healed have removed themselves from the sphere wherein he exercises power)—he even affects a transparently false democratic and benign pose,

---

dain at one of the world's less imposing pursuits. Do they retain (create) an image of me triumphantly plucking the pickle from the barrel and view it as unbridled and abhorrent male ego? Or is it the pickle from their barrel, a mastabatory male selfishness, a refusal of their good orifice? Nonsense, of course. But I am willing to leave open the option that my pickles are more than they seem.

[10] It may be that women in our society are particularly powerless because they are excessively probed and penetrated. There may well be no hope for them unless they change their anatomy—or unless men become equally probed and penetrated. Who sticks whom is a pervasive metaphor that describes essential power—fact. However, the sharp edges that have obtained in this configuration are becoming shadowed as penetration takes on increasingly varied guises. It is becoming quite possible for anyone to be "screwed," for example, at any time, in any place, in any way (or, as they say in the street of life's contretemps, "fucked over"). Certainly, then, it is not amiss to see the probing of doctors as a grand "screwing" on a metaphysical scale, with all attendant reverberations of power, sex, violation, etc. That is why men hate above all the sheathed proctological finger of prostate examinations, a double pronging. (But were it a woman?) I am indebted, in part, for these observations and some of the rhetoric to the weak child (a daughter) alluded to in endnote 7, with whom I argued these points before she left. Time and distance, however, have brought me closer to her view. It might even be that she is no longer frail; I have not seen her in three years. And time, I am told, works changes. It is even possible I am a grandfather! (It is even possible that she is near to me in space, however far in time, since we have not communicated!) Perhaps I have even seen her! (Why did she never like her dolls?)

healer to all mankind—because it eases the performance of his real activities; it is tradable in society. (In fact, he prefers, profoundly, for his patient to pay for his violation). This also explains the often deific posturing of the medical person, for as his methods of probing and penetrating increase, his sense of power deepens. The true motivation of doctors is Faustian, however stupidly so.[11] It is all, of course, a delusion, the seeking of a pearl at the heart of an onion.[12] The curative by-products of their probing increase, but at the furthest end, where penetration begins to double back on itself, is not power, certainly not knowledge, but empty space, the whiteness of Ahab's whale, frustration, rage, and

---

[11] A humorous parallel forced itself on me at this moment. I am aware that the reader might say to me, "And what are you, knifing with your naked arm into the briny pickle barrel? Do you not probe your own orifice?" Every man his orifice? Is that what you are telling me? Forgetting that it is already a long time since I had need to thrust my arm into a pickle barrel (I have risen modestly), let me say this: yes, it is true. There is a deep pleasure in plunging the pickle barrel, or amniotic brine, if you will. But all I seek is the birth of a firm, large sour pickle. Yes, I hold it up in a kind of dripping homunculoid triumph. But that is the end of it. I give it away (for money, to be sure). Someone else eats it, and I do not mind that at all. It is a material act, and to a degree an esthetic act. But that is all, whether you believe me or not. I seek no hidden, abusive end, whatever you may think of me psychologically. (And what of you, meat-cutter, shelver of dry books, gear-shifter, gas pumper, baker of loaves in ovens, hair-dresser and pedicurist, sewer of seams, and stuffer of chickens, turkeys, and geese!).

[12] I think the reader can see here that my early efforts at poetry were doomed to failure. Perhaps, had I kept a journal, I might have been more successful. But once I left off my studies to earn a living, I confess I did not think my life worth jotting down. Wrongly, I realize: the inner experience of all modes of earning a living is worth recording. But there are few to do it, and fewer means. The passage from birth to death is both boring (inconsequential) and of enormous interest.

possibly the despair which renders men children or lunatics, when confronted with the macrocosm that lurks within the minutest microcosm. After all that, there may be the beginning of true knowledge, or wisdom, but it is unlikely, for the acquisition of that knowledge requires a posture of humility, and power and humility are incompatible except perhaps in some few great men. Metaphysical strut glutinates the bones. Some of the great writers, as well as much popular literature, have recognized this essential if hidden aspect of the medical person. Hawthorne's Rappaccini, for example, whose probing cost him his daughter's life, or that same writer's Aylmer, who destroyed his wife to perfect her beauty. Both sought power through penetration, turned loved ones into objects.[13] Mad doctors, Cartesian maniacs, abound in the literature of the common man, and it must be seen that beneath the benign healing mask of most medical personnel is also the mad doctor of literature and comic books and nightmare who seeks

---

[13] Could Hawthorne even have written about a pickle wholesaler? (See endnote7) Does a pickle wholesaler have a soul? Does he experience the higher levels of torment? (Do women ever swoon over him?) These, despite appearances, are important questions. My daughter's name is Jenny. At this moment I have a suspicion that she might be robust, and my heart leaps at the thought at the same time that I smack my head for it. I think had I been more political in life, less metaphysical, I might have been happier. Marx could have loved a pickle-dealer, hedonistic as the pursuit might seem. But a pickle-dealer at the barricades? My comrades would have laughed as they died. Why can I never get rid of the aura of joke about my life? Is going to bed with a machine-tender or a stock broker or a shooter of guns any better? If at least I had a better set of teeth, smaller ears, if I drove well. I don't really ask for much.

your orifice. It is only in recent years that doctors have progressively weakened the mask of caring, healing person. The land cries out with their indifference to the individual as a person, cohabiter of the earth. But this is good also because it makes it more possible to see the doctor as he truly is, a prober and penetrator of our bodies for the acquisition of power, and to begin to see that what doctors *do* is indeed very strange, perhaps evil, and certainly infantile. We need therefore to ponder the society that promotes and lauds them, for unconsciously we *do* sense and permit what it is they really do; and we, therefore, are strange, too.[14] There is a deep schism in medicine in our land, and it widens. Into that gap we—our frail, heaving bodies and souls—fall.[15]

As I thought of this, wondering, to be sure, about the effect of my pretty pills, a further notion occurred to me (but I am

---

[14] i.e. We offer up our bodies to strange gods. Lordosis is fast becoming a (the?) universal metaphor. At moments like this my pickle-god seems like a teddy bear, benign beyond belief.

[15] It is perhaps too obvious to say that our great hospitals reflect all this demonism. They are huge machines that run our bodies, but they have lost sight of the individuals in the bodies in their metastasized bureaucracy. Whether I come as food, a body to be healed, oil to heat, or a toilet supply is all the same to them. But I have become philosophical. It is all pretty much the same everywhere. The butcher would hack off my arm without a second thought and wrap it up neatly for Mrs. Ginsberg, who would eat it talking about the weather to Mr. Ginsberg. Dogs defecate on my shoes while I am wearing them. I have already only narrowly escaped the rear end of the early morning sanitation truck. (And I would not have been the first). I have a new laugh for all this, and my wife thinks my brain is pickled. Just the other day someone called me a dirty kike. How anthropologically wondrous, how demented, how true. Thus does deeper reality impinge

not yet at my second thought for the day), and that is that several other of our most highly acclaimed professions share this quality with doctors, reinforcing a characteristic of our society. Dentists, of course (although objects of humor), who part lips and nakedly probe the oral cavity eight or ten hours a day.[16] There is less intensity here; they are fractional medical people. Nevertheless they are on the same continuum; despite their low status, limited operational area, and the fact that they literally and ridiculously spend the day with their fingers in other people's mouths, one can usually sooner or later detect in them the grim probing purpose, sometimes barely restrained (as when your breathing or the comfort and safety of your tongue are irrelevant to them),[17] as if by curing a tooth they seek to suture a pancreas.

---

in sudden ways. I am ready for a new Auschwitz.

[16] An amusing experiment for one is, when next introduced to a dentist at a social gathering, to say something like, "So. You work the oral orifice?" and see what reaction one gets. A few might be annoyed, but most, I suspect, will be gratified and begin to preen. "Mouth" is too aggressive a concept; it contains rataliatory power. But "oral orifice" is a passive passageway to deeper realms.

[17] I sensed, with one dentist, a refugee from Central Europe, I think, who spoke volubly but never clearly on the problems of my teeth, that he actually wanted me to take enemas before my visits. I say "sensed" because I could never understand him or his leering fat nurse-secretary. Perhaps he was not a dentist at all but more like a meta-dentist. I went to him originally out of some peculiar Whitmanian/Thoreauvian resolve, i.e., he was of my community, I could walk to him, it seemed simple, basic, direct, natural; he never sweetened his water. But the reality was more like some windowless, sweat-soaked, Balkan health club. Without benefit of passport I was instantly transported to murky realms with each visit. Fortunately, when I left the Bronx (for better things) I left

Kenneth Bernard

More interesting are the psychotherapists and their ilk, who probe the mind, whose instruments are words, particularly sharp-edged label-incantations like *manic, anal-retentive, fixation, phobic* (and sometimes drugs and quasi-medical techniques like hypnosis—as if we were not already hypnotized in this life) (Have you seen the new film, "The Invasion of the Anal-Retentives?"). Here also the patient is lying, and although not (usually) naked the patient often feels more vulnerable, more violated, more penetrated, more abandoned and isolated. He has had his soul scraped, like an aborted womb, and is left shivering and humiliated by the therapist's probe, lacking even the white, disposable mini-gown (really a disguised straitjacket: the ill are akin to the insane; only by controlling them can they be forgotten.)[18] (Question: why are *hunch-*

---

him also. But I also, over the years, have come to think I might have done him an injustice. His was perhaps a different paradigm from the doctors I am describing. Murky, yes, but not so much metaphysically as sensually, intellectually, and psychologically. He never, for example, had really clean hands. His clothes smelled of food and tobacco. His own teeth were irregular and stained. Also, he clearly respected his fat nurse. When they spoke in their language (and they spoke often and at length, as if all of life would not suffice to exhaust their subject), it was in terms of equality. He also thought her attractive. I heard recently that he had a stroke shortly after I left, that the woman nursed him with great devotion for ten years until he died. Were they lovers? And where is she now? And in what condition? I think I miss them. I have moved, in a sense, into the realms of light, but I am not happy there. I have something deeper than nostalgia for the chiaroscuro in which they lived, the shabby rooms in which we exchanged essential but odd services in grammarless language. My gums flourish but my soul languishes. Perhaps I should make a pilgrimage. (But where?)

[18] The ill also control themselves by reading medical dictionaries and such. Many a

*backs* so suited to the profession?) Finally there are the lawyers and accountants and such, who probe our financial and familial lives. It is increasingly difficult to move through life without them, and they demand, for their servicing, access to other deep and secret places of ourselves, like family mysteries or our dying words in advance of our death. No doubt there are more to be named, like certain political people and most of our social scientific fraternity, the mad scholar-epistemologists who vacuum "truth" perfectly, the burgeoning state *apparat* with its Frankenstein technology, experts who probe with statistics and studies and store the wombs and testicles they have collected in secret warehouses; but these suffice. They all share a detachment from the individual patient-client, subject-victim, a satisfaction in the probing-penetration in itself as a means of power. They are all equally deluded and shallow, and some of them are no doubt mad. In each of them there is a large component that tends to be hidden and unacknowledged. Unfortunately, even on the lower rungs of society's ladder—shop clerks, stamp-sellers, bank tellers, for example—we often feel the greedy fingers and squirm under probing eyes, wondering what penalty we are now to be subjected to and for what transgression.[19] Next to all of them the money-

---

person has lost his soul by discovering his illness. Nomenclature is both necessary and the enemy of freedom. Asthma has as many names as victims.

[19] I am fairly convinced that it is possible to smell these people out. Their cast of soul

making exprepreneur, the manic creators and producers of innumerable *things*, the makers of bombs and wars even, seem like a beam of light, even child-like. They are the laughers in the $80 seats at our musicals and comedies.[20] Not enmeshed are they in any deep drama of night. What is most interesting in all this is what it suggests about our society, a certain drift—that we have

---

cannot but infiltrate their bio-chemical systems. Hence their breath, their sweat, their body odors, even their urine and feces gave a distinctive, recognizable smell. Their clothing becomes impregnated with it, and their drapes, quilts, towels, and furniture. Finally, even their spouses and children, and the institutions they inhabit take on the smell. Hence, for example, a line like, "something is rotten in the state of Denmark." The rotting rat will always stink up the house. And so I say, look for those people with active noses, who seem to be smelling something unfamiliar and foul, vaguely threatening, awry. If they look fearful and posed for flight, so much the better. Follow them. The smell of burning bodies was present long before the ovens. One difference between my wife and me is that she has never allowed herself to understand my twitching nose. (See the latter portion of note #15) I think my absent daughter does, but her solutions, as I understand them, are puerile, simplistically political. (I have no faith in "the people," however much I might have in people). To look at the truth is to become uncompanionable, to lose a tooth with household pliers. It is bad for digestion, sex, parties, even life. It is also an unavoidable curse, like "reason" for an unchosen few.

[20] One might say that whatever cannot be turned into entertainment does not exist in our society. Hence we legitimize slavery and the Holocaust, ultimately, by singing about them, e.g.,
We're in the oven,
We're through with lovin',
But our spirits strong
Will conquer wrong—
NEVER SHALL WE DIE!
(They dance; I strangle my weeping neighbor)
Actually, we legitimatize also by commercial use: if we can sell something with it, it exists. Many an artist and work of art has been thus rescued from neglect and oblivion. In this respect, as a pickle-dealer, I am safe.

## The Man in the Stretcher

placed in positions of honor (and institutionalized and protected what they represent) a *type* of person whose real (secret) interest is not money, not his patient-clients in themselves, no ideal of service or utility to society or humanity, not even fame, but a devious violation of the individual, a vampirish probing and penetration, for the gaining of power, an unholy and soiled grail. It is not Machiavellian, not even psychopathological, but a metaphysical deformity, summed up in older times by the term evil.[21] It explains, I think, a great deal about our society, our so-called sense of victimization, for example, the listless bodies that litter our landscape. Something is out there getting at us. Ignorant and dirty fingers probe our souls. How refreshing seem the despoiler of women, the picker of pockets, the braggart, the liar, the bully. When next stretched out on the examining table (of whatever variety, naked beneath the thin sheet or inadequate gown,[22]

---

[21] Our art today lacks the dimension of evil. (It is still retained in politics, as in "the evils of capitalism," i.e.,—ironically—the godlessness of capitalism). Our art is morally neutral, technological, an hysteria of the minimal and the formal. When I listen (even) to Mozart, I feel archaic. A pickle wholesaler can listen to Mozart, but he is (almost by definition) not allowed receptivity to current forms. It is at times like these that I miss my parents and feel like weeping (not crying; weeping). They died too young! (From overwork). Pickle-dealers were once loved and respected (at least by their families), and when my parents lived I was connected with the world. (And almost to nature).

[22] Is there a reason for the gown's inadequacy? In my visits I have always realized the need for access to primary orifices. But the exposure and vulnerability of my sexual parts has always disturbed me. ("When this gown you wear, your cock is mine!"). There is always inadvertant frottage. And what am I supposed to do when his nurse or (as twice happened) his secretary walks in? To become erect would surely be an embarrass-

awaiting the probing, then penetrating fingers and instruments, watch the eyes, try to ignite the flame of human communion, smell the burning brain, note the poised orgasmic hand, ask yourself—Do I exist or not? Am I being healed or used? Who (what) is this strange creature? What does he seek through me? Why is he *powerful* and I powerless? Who has decreed this relationship? Why must there be *pain, anxiety, abandonment*? And can I (we) survive it?

\* \* \* \*

My second drugged thought for the day, much briefer, begins with an observation by a well known critic and veers off into fantasy, I suppose. Several years ago, in a book whose title referred to Bluebeard, the author noted that one of the things lost forever by the killing of the Jews in World War II was the gene-pool they represented. Forever more, no children would be conceived from that cluster of humanity, and whatever talents and

---

ment, even though they would overlook it, professionals that they are. (A professional is one who ignores the gratuitous erections of life.) Yet not to do so, to lie there limply exposed in my medical tutu (a new art form comparable to Dada), seems a manly failure. A proper solution, of course, would be for us all to wear the same inadequate garment. Or if I were allowed to bring and let loose on the premises my pet pigeon or monkey. A frisky and nosy monkey would more than compensate for testicles at risk, especially if he were goosing everybody.

achievements that would have been uniquely theirs would never be made manifest in history.[23] That enormity, that absoluteness, of loss has since haunted me, comparable, I suppose, to the properties of all the unique unexamined flora and fauna that yearly disappear forever from the earth in the march of progress.[24] We seem to be in a downward spiral whose end is better not imagined. And then, just the other day, I read something of medical achievement that made me sad because of its tardiness but also oddly hopeful. A French woman, whose husband had died of testicular cancer only a few days after their marriage, was granted, after prolonged legal battle, impregnating use of sperm her former husband had wisely frozen several years before in anticipation of future sterility and possible death.[25] The woman was, she said, relieved and

---

[23] Do not think I am mindless of how this pickle-wholesaler would figure in such a gene-pool. However, my wife is the ugly older daughter of a rabbi who was the son of a rabbi, and that should count for something should our frail child ever have issue.

[24] It is obvious that eventually art will invent most, maybe all, of our animal and plant life (W. Disney has made a good start). And this is comforting because then it will be immortal. It will also clothe us (our psyches) rather than merely surround us. This solipsistic world will be a new paradise, wherein will be no need to seek names for things, for we shall have invented them already. At that point we shall also banish death as a weakness of former ages and become immortal ourselves.

[25] How French of him to leave her his sperm. Myself, of different persuasion, I would have left my money and property—and I no sooner say it than I am chagrined. How crass. How unromantic. How stupid. Why not my old shoes as well? It was interesting that France being a Catholic country, there was some reluctance to grant her wish because at the time he banked his sperm she was merely his mistress, not wife; her egg (fertilized) would not have been sanctified by the sacrament of marriage, i.e., her current ovulations were post-marriage and his sperm were pre-marriage. Had his sperm

full of joy that a dream could be realized through the miracle-seeming new medical technology. And I thought, *what a difference it would have made* had all those Jews (all those Poles, Russians, Gypsies, *Jehovah's Witnesses*), before being gassed and shot and starved and beaten to death, been able to deposit sperm in banks (like money that will accrue interest), with basic information about each stored in micro-chips. Then, even though dead these fifty, one hundred, or thousand years, their sperm might have been matched with young awaiting wombs (Volunteers for the Future), and new generations marched, so to speak, from the grave itself, thus uniting old suffering and loss with new vigor and hope.[26] How mitigated, then, it might all have been, the loss

---

been frozen during the actual days of his marriage, the problem might not have arisen, or at least been less complex, i.e., how illicit would the union of a widow's egg with a dead husband's sperm be? This subject obviously begs further development. For example, one can envision aged children, childless themselves, mating the sperm and egg of long dead parents to create younger siblings to inherit their wealth. Or a single nuclear couple continuing to produce offspring for a century or more, be they idiot or genius. One can even foresee a dynastic future in which no living person need ever procreate, so vast the frozen heritage of sperm and egg awaiting election. Suitable bearer-bodies will always (for a living wage) be available from whatever third world exists. And lawyers also to unravel rights, procedures, precedence, and liabilities. But these bureaucratic matters are beyond the scope of this fiction, so enough.

[26] For the legal or religious purists we might carry our French precedent a step further. Who is to say a woman cannot or may not marry a dead man? If his sperm lives, so lives he. Let a woman choose from the living *and* the dead, and if a man, even a pickle wholesaler, should choose to leave his estate along with his sperm, why so much the better for the woman who seeks to raise his children. A woman, we now realize, does not need a man. She needs a friend perhaps. And sometimes she might need a sperm as

es cut so dramatically, green fields across the desert years. What generations might yet have arisen. And how great, today, in our modern world, the retrieval of error, as from radical shifts of political power or even capital punishment (See the condemned man depositing his sperm with a smile), with such technology. Preparatory to any armed conflict or extermination, for example, might well be compulsory storage of sperm (and even egg! with suitable warning), so that, though bodies fall, though individual life be truncated, the future might live in its full amplitudes. No tyrant, then, without his measure of redemption. Away the troubled thoughts of Gulag and camp, jungle slaughter, dungeon, and bureaucratic treacheries! Onward without essential loss! What, then, would the critic say of lost genepools? Am I possibly feeling, as I grow drowsy, the excitement, the passion, the *triumph* of penetration? Medical man, lawyer, scientist, administrator, probers *all*—do I owe you an apology?

Endnotes

Although I have felt all along that formal notes would not be necessary for this piece, it turns out there are several:

    1.    Although it is clear that a large component of what doctors, etc., really seek is power of an unattractive

---

well. There is a new romanticism on the horizon. Let blushing girls picnic in crumbling cemeteries.

kind, they are not as materially rewarded for their function as are those who baldly seek wealth and the power it confers or those who seek power first (as in a military or political eminence) and the wealth it confers.[27] This, on the whole, though often deadly, is healthy, or healthier. There is little that is secret about such men and their desires (Compare, for example, the wives of such men with those of doctors),[28] and their grossness, although often barbaric (electric devices in selected orifices, nipple-amputation), is usually idiosyncratic, cultural (ideological), socio-pathological, at worst clinical rather than metaphysical.[29] They are almost entirely visible as what they are (e.g., Destroy the capitalists! Let the buyer beware! Hang the wrong-thinkers!). Doctors and such, on the other hand, are invisible in their metaphysical programme. They are rewarded for what they are least interested in—healing individuals—not for their secret, necromantic goals, which are not simple and not (particularly) material. Our society values material power most, but it is the seekers of

---

[27] Among whom naturally I do not count myself. No stretch of imagination can conceive of anyone in the pickle business aspiring to power. My livelihood, I know, has been a disappointment to my wife, so rabbi-conscious. Had it perhaps been a springboard to higher achievement, to more money, a proper desk, to power, she might have become reconciled to it. There was never any way that I could tell her about the pickle barrel stink that lingered on the hands. Of such stink is destiny limned.

[28] It has been my personal observation that medical wives tend towards the mousy, drink more, are less educated and healthy, and are less erotic then the wives of other professionals. They simply do not know what they have gotten themselves into. I'm not entirely sure what this means, except that over the years there is a great wearing away in them and a haunted look that sees from within a void.

metaphysical power who may threaten it more. We may prevent, circumvent, possibly even survive bombs and the destruction of our environment (in however attenuated a form, say with six legs), but there will be no "we" if we are despoiled of our souls.

2. Nurses are fundamentally different from doctors in that their entire goal is comforting and healing.[30] That is why patients relate far better to nurses than to doctors. There is no hidden factor, no residual anxiety or fear. Nurses attend completely to the needs of the individual patient and derive all their satisfaction and fulfillment from those acts (Has

---

[29] Cultures do differ on the infliction of pain. Some Indians of old, I have read, heaped hot coals on the scalped heads of still living prisoners, who often laughed in contempt. In some of the more picturesque parts of the New World severed scrotums are routinely stuffed into oral cavities, a potent demographic and reproductive symbolism. The collection of eyeballs from dead soldiers for soup by an infamous Balkan general of yesteryear seems quaint by modern standards. I feel bold enough to suggest that, in this area, we pickle-dealers are harmless folk. There is nothing in the handling of pickles to promote cruelty. I think I may say that a nation of pickle-dealers would not be such a terrible thing. A little brine in the eye never hurt anyone.

[30] Perhaps I should say, "used to be," and what follows should temper the above. Except in the provinces, there has been a marked shift, perhaps unavoidable in our hard times, from a quasi-religious calling to a mostly economic one. This parallels a racial and ethnic shift from the Celtic and Anglo-Saxon to the darker-skinned. The former, in their crisp white chirpiness seemed almost without essential orifice, prelapsarian, commendably devotional to my needs. The latter, no less skilled, are clearly earning a living, redressing the inequities of the world, and fulfilling orificial needs elsewhere. I confess to mixed, and probably embarrassing, feelings on the subject and admit that what I say about nurses is probably more the lingering dream than the fact, which is that nursing is good business for some people. However, the image in peoples' minds dies hard. They do not yet see the cold cash look that precedes the enema.

anyone ever seen a doctor empty a bed-pan or bring a glass of water to a patient? What patient, however urgent the need, would even dare to ask his doctor for a glass of water? And how many would bring it, rather than direct that it be brought?) It goes without saying that nurses (whether old or new variety) should not marry doctors but rather businessmen, teachers, bus drivers, laborers, etc., unless they have a need to be unhappy.[31] Second level medical people, i.e., the technicians (among whom I number pathologists), are also fundamentally different, but their primary interest may not be the needs of the individual patient but rather their machines. They rarely seek anything further than the smooth functioning of their machines, e.g., a good x-ray or tissue slide, even if of cancer, is fulfillment enough; given scope enough, they would find a good gassing sufficient, too.[32]

3. Lawyers who function mainly for the relief of individuals, especially those without status, celebrity,

---

[31] Looking at my wife sometimes I am aware that I cannot conceive of a rabbi's daughter as a nurse. (Yet she nurses me well when I am ill.) That a rabbi's daughter, or for that matter a Hungarian or a Serbo-Croat, cannot easily be conceived as a nurse adumbrates some subtle hierarchy or truth. My wife was never a sportswoman either. The world has changed so fast. Though still among the quick, I sense a mausoleum smell about me. I am convinced younger people than I have naturally better breath than I. I peek too long at young women.

[32] The gassing trucks in the early stages of Jewish resettlement were exquisitely designed by earnest men in clean shirts. For example, the concealed drainage hole on the floor was slanted and enlarged to accommodate quick evacuation of vomit, urine, and feces of the distressed occupants.

power, or money, are the least rewarded and least respected by their peers and by society, too. The penetration potential is low among unwashed and residual bodies. In this respect they are more akin to nurses and nuns than doctors and are fundamentally alienated from their fraternity. (Other lawyers twitch their noses in their presence, as if they carried feces on their cuffs).

4. This is not, however, similarly true of lower-echelon psychotherapists—counselors, guidance people, social workers, advisors. Although they lack the self-esteem and the approbation of their professional superiors, they seek the same goals, but with less finesse.[33]

5. At one point I have described what doctors do as infantile. What I mean is this. A child feels helpless in the world and seeks, as he ages, to extend his mastery over it. But to become adult is to limit this goal, to realize the futility of mastery and settle for imperfection, irresolvable dialog, mystery.[34] Some infants never become adults. But instead of contin-

---

[33] Among the people mentioned here and just above I have noticed a less stringent dress code. Non-probers indulge themselves more with color and stylistic mismatching. Whether it has to do with love of life and flaccid self-delusion or insecurity and low self-image is difficult to say. One advantage of my own arena of vocational pursuit is that there is no dress code at all except perhaps the rolled-up sleeve and sometimes an apron.

[34] I do not mean to imply by this that we must become as babes in the lap of the Almighty. No. The imperfection I speak of has no consolation, no transcendant resolution. It is rather an unhealable wound that is co-existent with life. Death alone cures. Life is the sickness.

uing to throw tantrums they channel their frustrations and goals into societally "edifying" discourse like "doctoring."

6. (A sub-note, really) The doctors I have been speaking of are profoundly Protestant. This is a late insight, mysterious, and really beyond my ken except to say (again) that some tinkering with the infernal is involved. Dr. Mengele may be a prototype here.

7. Finally, myself. I showed these scribbles to one of the few people I speak meaningfully with these days (my druggist). He said it would give more panache (that was his word) to what I had written if I added a few formal details of my character and life. Actually, I don't agree, but I prefer to err on the side of caution (always). I am, as you can guess, definitely on the declining side of life. It pains me to look at just about anything, yet I am forever looking. I married late and although I am comfortable, as far as material needs (I am in the wholesale pickle business, despite a somewhat scholarly youth), my life has a gray, meager quality. We had one (weak) child, who wandered off early.[35] I am not prepossessing. I wear thick glasses, but have a full head of hair. I expect to die

---

[35] As a late youth, I had one passionate affair with a dark curly-haired immigrant from the Near-East, which I was subsequently told, resulted in a child. But since I have never heard from either, it is irrelevant. I put it in only as a fact for the punctilious, of whom I am not one. Attentiveness to detail is a delusion. Details are always the servants of orthodoxy. True freedom is pain.

before my time, if not from illness and anxiety, then from confusion and boredom. My only fantasy (once) was to have lived the life of a perfect pickle, from fecund earth to embalming barrel to greedy mouth.[36] That makes sense to me. Nothing else is suitable for a note, and, indeed, there would be little more even for a novel.

7A.   I am perhaps too scrupulous. I confess to a well-suppressed hopefulness over mankind. This can be seen occasionally in my walk, which can be jaunty. Yet, at the same time, I have never wanted to own a pet, mainly because they get sick and die.[37] At any rate, the time for pets was earlier in my life. Now I look at the pets of other people and get a grim satisfaction from it.

7B.   (I use parenthesis because I am feeling the impulse to submerge again. Disguise equals longevity. I am aware of the frequency with which I urge the reader to return to this endnote, and I feel it might, finally, disappoint him. Hence a revelation or two more. My mother had one miscarriage that I know of. And although he/she was never discussed he/she was a presence in our home in the early years and a psychic companion to me, embodying both past and future, potentiality, conscience, and

---

[36] "Mouth" here I am obviously viewing as a metaphor, possibly even a hopeful metaphor, e.g., God as consumer of pickles.

[37] A dog or cat or canary that would live one or two hundred years, that is, outlive me, would be acceptable. My grandchildren, then, could conceivably romp with an animal that knew their grandpa when he was a child. That might be a comfort for them and possibly to me: i.e., handing down the dog that knew me to my heirs

anxiety. Somewhere around my delayed adolescence, that presence metamorphosed into something else, something which, although more vague, put a stamp on my life, a stamp which gave me no joy but infinite endurance against the foibles and mystery of life. A second revelation: for a year and a half as a young adult, I secretly fed an alley cat named—by me—Minnie. She was killed by a car, and I left her in the gutter, although I cried over her loss several nights.)

8.   A late addition, consequent on rereading footnote #10 and no doubt sexist but nevertheless true: all that has been said pertains, as yet, only to men. Women who are doctors are fundamentally different. This might, however, change. (See endnote #2 and footnote #26, for example). Too complex, I think, to deal with. Perhaps related to endnote #6.

9.   (Or 7C) The absolute finish: I do not like pickles. (Neither is my wife really ugly.)

## EX FACTO ORITUR IUS*

Let us take the eye, the transparent eye, the eye that *sees* without obstruction. The child misbehaves. All children misbehave. The law, then, says discipline and punish. Or should it be reversed? To all this I say, "Whose eye is this? Where does such innocence exist?" Perhaps for one moment after we are born, the eye sees. But it does not record. It cannot record. The eye, for that one moment, is also what it sees. The event passes through, but goes nowhere. Thereafter, the eye sees, but always, of course, according to something else. Our first moment is all we will ever know of paradise. Thereafter, the eye loses transparency. Lizards of all sizes enter the brain. But who would want a life of paradise, a life of nothingness? Perhaps a holy man or a fool.

What comes of all this, of course, is that the law is a fraud. Because, barring that pristine first moment, there can never be a true account of the fact (and if there were, it could only be meaningless); there can be no law worthy of the name. I have tried to

---

*"It is from the true account of the fact that the law is born"

explain this to my wife, but to no avail. Our child still gets spanked. He is crying, and I sit pondering the true nature of his transgression. I know this will continue. Our son will progress from punishment to punishment and will finally achieve a personality, all resting on a sea of mud. Meanwhile, the dishes get regularly done, the house is cleaned, the bills paid. There is courage in all this. I laugh a reasonable amount and grow older. I know I am going to die, and nothing in that prospect beckons me except possibly that there might be a second moment of transparency, a moment when, gifted with a lifetime of language and experience, I might say to my wife (she will outlive me, of course; law-makers live long lives), "Why, here is how it is. This is what I see. Construct your law upon this."

But would she hear me? Would I be speaking a language she understood? For it occurs to me that I could speak to her in no familiar terms. Hearing my gibberish, she would cry all the more at the loss of my mental function. And yet, if she could have the presence of mind to record my babble, she might in time learn, by listening to it, to be wise. But I have loved her dearly, and in pity for her pain, I finally utter, "*Melius esse quam videri*," "Better to be than to seem." Futile, of course, and no doubt a compromise, but she is an old Latin student (her earliest charm) and will smile at this. It will be a good way to go out.

Meanwhile, our son has become, of all things, a man of

the law. Of course I take pride in this. In his early days, full of enthusiasm, he talks a lot with me. I look at him very seriously. Later, we talk less. He seems impatient with me. Perhaps he senses the wild laughter I hold in check, and his success in the law is also his revenge. Some laughter simply cannot be borne. Of course, he also has friends and colleagues to keep him busy. The world occupies him. And I have to admit I appear increasingly useless. When I am mugged, I can summon up no anger. Wars come and go for me. I appear to watch traffic with great interest. Of course I continue to work. I even prosper. My wife has great forbearance, and we still have jolly times. I am grateful that she is healthy, that she reads a great deal, even that she is active in fomenting good works.

 I, in contrast, get a dog and name him Cassandro. We take long walks and converse a lot. Always, my eye is looking, and I am doubting what it sees. I am an unreliable witness. Is my dog wetting your leg? Impossible to say. Gradually I realize that my wife considers me some kind of fool, but perhaps a holy fool. I don't mind that. I even smile at it. I take it as a kind of recognition, and we get along better than ever. Unexpectedly we have another child, a girl, whom we agree to name Phoebe. Perhaps because my wife is now older, she disciplines her less, even than I. She has become a great *interpreter* of Phoebe's actions, and more, and soon we are all four (I include Cassandro) scurrying over the landscape, jabbering away. Phoebe speaks baby talk. Cassandro barks a thousand interesting ways. And my wife and I—we speak, joyfully, with total indirection and silliness. I have never been happier.

And then I get sick. Such things happen in life. Somehow my wife thinks it is a punishment (according to something or other) and reverts to her old ways. Our son is very useful. He sees us as quite old and in need of proper care. I love him very much and let him tend me. Perhaps it is not yet the end. I try to enjoy what I have. What I have, most days, is this. I lie in a clean bed. My pain is bearable. My wife sits by the bed, not yet crying. Mainly she watches (probably for a sign of sense). A small, wild-eyed girl comes in and out of the room for no apparent reason, although sometimes she touches the blanket covering me. Cassandro sits in a corner scratching and sleeping. I have already formulated my expectation of a final moment of clear vision. I look at my wife and smile. The time is passing. I am content.

## VINES

Lately I notice that I *smell* more. I used to be able to wear the same shirt three or four days without being aware of it. Now, even in the course of a day, it smells foul. *I* smell foul. It doesn't seem to matter whether or not I take cosmetic precaution. My *deodorants* smell foul by the end of the day. Along with this my feet are getting colder and sweating differently. My blood is circulating less. I think about my teeth a lot. Not too long ago I used to begin days feeling on top of things. Lately I realize I'm full of little stratagems to hold it all together. I wiggle a toe here, take an extra breath there, tighten my buttocks inconspicuously on the subway. I asked my wife recently whether or not she ever got that rotten fruit feeling, that sense of galloping inner deterioration before falling from the vine with a sickening *plush*. She answered quickly and emphatically, as befits a Vassar girl: "No," she said, "I don't. I get tired. I get headaches. I get disgusted. And I get periods." There was a pause. "*Sometimes*," I said, repaying her for the speed and emphasis of her answer. She cackled. All things considered, she wasn't bad.

Not so my friend Norman. "What do you mean, that rotten

fruit feeling?" he said. Norman is a health culturist. He does a lot of yoga and eats well. He impresses people as having a clean system. "Look," he said. "Maybe *you've* got to go, but *I* don't." I wondered whether he had moved on to something besides yoga. "I've told you for years," he said, "that you are literally full of rotten shit." I don't really like talking to Norman. For one thing, he never knows what I'm talking about. But my wife and his went to elementary school together. I'm really waiting for him to get a hernia before I talk to him seriously. I have several friends like Norman.

    It actually comes down to the fact that I can talk to my wife best of all. Not that I don't make her sick a lot. But we've been together twenty-five years. That kind of thing is stronger than just about anything. Who else, for example, knows how many inconsequential and humiliating things my body has been through?" "Look," she said, "the fact is that you're going to die sooner or later. Some bodies are in better shape for it than others." "Norman isn't really so dumb. What kind of shape is Marie in?" Marie is Norman's wife. "Do you really want to know?" she said. "Well, yes. Why not?" "She thinks she might have cancer. She's having a biopsy Tuesday." "My God," I said. My wife has a way of shortening my conversations. It's not just that she's a busy and successful woman. Through inadvertence or intent she frequently misconstrues my words just to that extent that I cannot respond to what she says. I am very subtly confused. I used to consider it girlish charm, but I don't anymore. It rather upsets me. I met Norman later in the week of his wife's biopsy. He practically hugged me. "Listen," he said, "why don't you start working out?" He looked at me with a lot of pain in his eyes, as if it was really important. "Norman, I'm really in a hurry," I said, moving off. "We'll talk about it." From half a block he shouted: "She's all right! She's all right!" It was all I could do not to run.

      Two days later, for reasons totally beyond me, I felt like a heart-to-heart talk with my wife. *Her* name is Edna. "Listen," I began auspiciously, "I realize we're *both* going to die." She stared at me. "And I want you to know it's all right." Her mouth opened, but she didn't speak. "I mean, the children, the twenty-five, or thirty, or…years, I mean, let me say something ridiculous…I just want you to know that I love you." Having spoken with my usual clarity, I was about to speak again. But she forestalled me. "Will you please *shut up*!" I did.

## COLUMBUS DAY

A sad day. On my mother's side my family goes back to a village near Fano in Italy. But because my mother married out of the ethnic fold I cannot sport a Sannicandro or a Mancinelli. In addition to which my father once chased my mother's sister onto a fire escape with a butcher's knife: I have bad blood in me. My aunt feeds me gorgeously but she still stutters when she talks about it. I may look like my Uncle J. (I think it best to abbreviate), but there is no doubt that as I get older the strangeness is showing. My aunt, let us say Aunt I., is fat, pink, and excitable. And a small town girl. Stuttering on a Third Avenue fire escape must surely have been a high point in her nightmares. My Uncle J. was a favorite of mine. He spent most of his time in the cellar. He also taught me how to chop wood. His great feat in my childhood was the fearless poking of his arm into spider holes. Later, in Latin I, I read about the roman Lucius Scaevola. When captured by the enemy and threatened with torture he stuck his right hand in the fire and said, "Call me Lefty." My Uncle J. had a fraternal twin who ultimately became a hobo and lost a leg hitching a freight. However, they both left me with an interesting symbology of life. Meanwhile my Aunt I. is stuttering on the fire escape. There is a song in the Catskills of yore to the effect that all over Italy they sing so prettily (or in Napoli so happily) which makes me feel the curse of my doomed blood. My mother once drank cabbage juice for two weeks and tried to cure her sinus by having thumbs stuck up her nose. And my Uncle H. once didn't like the way my Aunt T. sang while washing dishes and didn't speak to her for two years. My Uncle T., whose wife wouldn't see or speak to him when she was dying of cancer, used to ride down hills standing on his motorcycle. Aunt N. wishes her husband's grave filled with horse manure, and Aunt I. unplugs all her appliances when she goes to work. I think it was summer when she was sweating on the fire escape. The colossal outrage of it. All my mother's family are superb cooks, and I see her staring and stuttering in at me in my dreams. She is saying something like, "You b-b-b-be a g-g-g-good boy." And I think I've tried. On this, Columbus Day, I try to overcome the bad blood in me by thinking of Columbus, Garibaldi, Machiavelli. I try to sing so happily, as they must have, of spider holes, cancer, stumps, and graves. But the cellar is dank, and monsters lurk behind the furnace. In the attic my Uncle M. dropped cigarette butts into his pot of urine and water until all hours of the night, and my Uncle H. went to sea. In the winter I rolled a hot brick in newspaper to put at the bottom of my bed. My Uncle J. once got a bald head but no one knew it for three weeks because he never took his hat off. The war came, and things fell apart. Everybody got older. My grandmother, who had twelve children, died at eighty-nine, blood spilling from the mouth all over her chest. And I sing.

# FISH EYE

I realize that it is a commonplace to think people are bumping into one. Indeed, that paranoia is at the heart of some of our finest modern works. By paranoia I do not, of course, mean anything crassly clinical or egoistic. No, I mean that pervading sense of conspiracy about one, that dread of some terrible thing impending, with no mediation possible. I respect that. I can share something of that. Let the thousand witless idiots in the street shrug off invisible offenders and tsk themselves into eternity. I have nothing to do with them, except to avoid their insult and violence. My complaint is somewhat different. I say *somewhat* because I do occasionally have inklings of brute actions and rude words in me, and, more often, I do feel intimations of a conspiracy rushing to its dread end. Let me try to be explicit. I am tempted to say right off that I am magnetic, that some ineffable and original power resides in me which draws people to me. But not in the way of ordinary human concourse. No. Rather it is like the pull of iron filings to their natural center. In effect, people actually bump into me. I say it straight out. I am a force people cannot resist, for whatever reason. I am reluctant to pursue this at the moment because I realize it might sound *strange*. And the bumping, which is of all varieties, from the merest brush to gull swoop to collision, would require some immediate philosophical grounding. For example, questions like "Who am I?" and "Why am I here?" would arise. I am not ready yet to deal with them. So let me, rather, crabwise creep up to them. That is always my preference. And immediately, then, I can cite what I choose to call "the fishy look." I have long wondered about that expression. For example, is it the look of a live or dead fish? The latter, I think, most definitely the latter. Now this look, the dead fish eye look, is not a bump. But it is often the prelude to a bump. I say "often" because although I encounter it frequently, I can never be certain that a bump will follow. Sometimes it is a mere predatory look, an assessment, I think, of a victim. The deadness is mere subterfuge. It says, "Don't worry. I neither see you nor intend to ravage you. Pretend I am not here." Of course, I do no such thing. The eye of a shark could not be more obvious to me. I allow myself a special tic I have cultivated, which communicates awareness. And that is that. Mr. Predator must look elsewhere. I am not his victim. However, there are some dead fish looks that are not a prelude to predation. They are my concern here. For with them there is almost a certainty of subsequent contact. The dead eye here is window to a dead interior, and such bodies are flung to me as to a lodestone. They find their home in me. Now that would be a disturbing revelation were it the sum of my collisions, that is, myself as the natural home of all the dead fish eye people in public places. But it is not the sum. I receive my fishy looks elsewhere than in public places. In my work place, for example. My colleagues frequently have the dead fish eye look for me. This is more difficult for me to incorporate. For some of my colleagues are almost distinguished. They trade in various intellectual matters, like the true ends of society or the nature of merit, which give testimony to interior life. And they never actually collide with me. But I feel the collision nevertheless. And that is important. A psychic collision is no less a collision. Indeed, I am sometimes so furious as to want to rip their limbs from their bodies, saying, "You wish to dissimulate? There, now dissimulate all you wish!" It is possible I have laughed a few times while having such thoughts. This is not as mad as it sounds. No doubt many people have such impulses in their work places. The work place is a jungle, a pit. Blood is let there regularly. There is ample testimony to this, numerous hanging bodies. However, by itself, this would not credit the magnetism of which I am speaking, my personal magnetism. Let us take the home instead. Yes, I have a home! A wife and children. At one point we had an animal. Sometimes I think that all that is remarkable. I am, after all, an unusual person. Nevertheless, once, we were indeed like happy squirrels, if one can impose such a condition. What squirrel, after all, is ever happy? What I mean is that once we appeared to live without perturbations. And then, quite overnight, as it were, my home became filled with dead fish eye looks. My wife, my children, woke up with them. I sensed that my nearest and dearest were slowly gravitating toward me, that I was their ultimate repository of deadness, and when they collided with me, like meteors to earth, I should scream and then expire. What dark night was that, you may well ask? I don't know. A home should be a sanctuary, I agree. Nevertheless, one night I went to sleep in what I took to be a sheltered world. And in the morning, I awoke to dread. It is a terrible burden I bear, for what can be the meaning and purpose of so many bodies being pulled into me? And speaking of my children, let me mention young people in general. Young people, by and large, do not have dead fish eyes. Yet they frequently collide with me. Now, at first I discounted the collisions. Young people are effervescent, full of life, busy with their own trivial concerns. They have no time to see who is in their way, to weave and twist in social accommodation. No, their path is straight, and let the standers beware. Let others dodge and quicken their steps. Youth must be served, even if others are trampled. But then, one day when I had been most harshly knocked, I looked over my shoulder to see who it was had bruised me. And there, yes, there, was the same dead fish eye look of which I have been speaking, implanted in a half-turned head that rested on a mass of young flesh. I knew then, with that Parthian glance, that something was afoot, that indeed there was scope to my magnetism. Somehow I had become the source of even greater magnitude than I had thought. I suppose I had somehow discovered fate, or at least my fate. And with that recognition there came also a sense of power. I feel, more than ever, that I need not be merely the passive recipient of collision, but that I can command it, will it. Crash unto me, ye meager beings, for I am your source. And with that has begun a small diminution of my dread. One thing bothers me, however, perhaps two. The first is the increasing appearance of men, and some few women, older, like me, who seem to be waiters and watchers upon my collisions. I have never noticed them before. They do not have the dead fish eye look; they will not bump into me. If anything, they have sad eyes. And they appear to have some intelligence service, for whenever collision is imminent, as is increasingly the case, they are there, silently witnessing. They do not appear to take any pleasure in what they see, but neither is there any compassion or awe. Sometimes I think they are waiting for me to speak to them, to join them somehow. But for what? What am I expected to say? Why should I join them? The second worrisome thing I alluded to earlier. Although I now have a firm sense of my magnetism, of others' irresistible need to lurch into me, to partake of my essence, perhaps, I do not yet have any firm grasp of what the essence is, of who, exactly I am or why I am here. I reject out of hand that I am, even in a small way, the Messiah, or a messiah. It is possible that I am a freak of nature, however, something the eons have spewed forth for some as yet undefined evolution or compensation. And it is possible that I am fulfilling a purpose in some higher plan, whose structure and end will in time be revealed to me, if I have courage and faith, even as I lie flat on the pavement. For I do, somehow, see myself, finally, lying on the pavement. Perhaps that is what the watchers and waiters are there for, to remind me of destiny, whatever that is. If that is the case, then they will find me resolute and worthy. For there cannot be many more steps to go. My body's accumulated history is large. Indeed, sometimes, just lately, my lips have been formulating what I think are the right words for them, the words that will explain, conclude, perhaps even thrill. I look forward to them. My mouth is juicy for them. But what, just yesterday, I was wondering, will be *their* words to me. If they are something like "This way, please" or "Follow us," I shall be disappointed. I might garble, strangulate my words. But perhaps that will be short-sighted of me. Perhaps their language will have to be interpreted. Perhaps it is a new language, which I shall have to learn, a post-collision language in keeping with my new estate. And then, of course, seeing the light, I shall follow willingly.

# UMBRELLA MAN

I have a philosopher friend who reports that he was chided recently by a distinguished colleague as to whether there were questions before as well as after breakfast. It was, of course, a friendly taxonomic query, perhaps just a little bit wicked. It says a good deal of my friend that he not only remembered, but repeated, the query. He clearly saw the pointedness of it. For he reported further that, for him, categories, if appropriate, can help organize things. One wonders, of course, which things would be so organized (and which things not) and by which appropriate categories. Taxonomy, clearly, is not only history, but life itself. And there are many busy little ants clarifying matters for the rest of us. For we all desperately need clarification. At the same time, we must be willing, I think, to consider how our world might be rearranged if, say, the liver were to usurp the heart as the seat of our passions, as the master organ and metaphor of life, and so on.

Much of the import of these matters was brought home to me recently by another friend, a big sausage of a dog named Mitzi. Mitzi, no philosopher, but possibly a philosopher dog, lies outside the house near my mailbox a quarter of a mile down the road. Being, as we say, neglected, she eagerly awaits my twice a day visits for regular pettings. She knows that Sunday, when there is no mail pickup, is some kind of anomaly, but not sufficient to disrupt her universe. Sometimes, for fun, I try to creep up to the mailbox without Mitzi's knowledge. But the least foot-scrape, the least pebble kicked, the least creak of the mailbox hinge and she is there, trembling, for her petting. Sometimes I think I am succeeding, getting away, back up the road, only to hear a huffing and puffing behind me. It is fat Mitzi, wanting her due, secure in the parameters we have established. She has no problem with my "game." It no doubt adds considerable zest to her life.

One day, however, things changed a bit, or perhaps quite a bit. In my own little world, the outgoing mail *must* go in the mailbox, no matter what (Sunday is a manageable anomaly for me also), for some sort of life depends on it. So despite the rain, I set off for the box, but with a large umbrella. Mitzi saw me early and went into her alarm mode—unfamiliar object approaching, systemic threat on the horizon. When I got close enough, I began my usual conversation with her, and soon all was mended, adjustments were made. But for a few moments I was aware of a taxonomic flurry, a furious tinkering, in her dog-brain. Did the rain change my form? Were umbrellas friendly? Was this another creeping-to-the-mailbox game? I don't know, exactly, how Mitzi resolved the matter. But the possibilities loomed large for me, particularly in the area of "appropriate categories." Was umbrella-man a new category or simply an anomaly like Sunday or a game variation like creeping-to-the-mailbox? Mitzi got her petting, and I resumed my human-brain life.

    How to sort it all out. Always. What if, for example, one day Mitzi were kicked by a creature under another umbrella. Why should I, on a subsequent rainy day, be bitten because someone had an argument with his wife? Categories have results. Taxonomies clash. Mitzi's world, I could see, was a complicated one, and I sympathized with her fully. Good as her nose was, it could not account for everything. Nor mine. On another occasion, my philosopher friend and I were discussing the contingencies of economic life. Although of some sort of Marxist persuasion, he was deeply invested in the stock market as the only insurance against an insecure and undignified old age in a hostile world. It was, he said, the common wisdom—slaving Chinese peasants, global decay, and so on notwithstanding. And there were experts to guide one, just as did doctors, for example, in the economies of the body. "Money invested," he said, "is like being on a life raft that goes up and down. Those not investing are like people stranded on a nearly deserted island." It was, I thought, a rather charming and dramatic metaphor. But how deserted could the island be with all those Chinese peasants on it? And metaphors, I thought further, were, like Mitzi's categories, slippery items. "We should be aware," I declared, "of the comfort of metaphors. For example, 'That's the way the ball bounces.' Said, or thought, just after one's throat has been slit."

We had a good laugh over that. Our talk drifted off into more mundane items, like when it was best to dig horse radish. Eventually his raft moved on, over the roiling ocean. Legs spread for a sense of balance, he waved to me, on my tiny island, crowded with peasants holding knives. I thought of Mitzi, facing her umbrella-man, or of myself, facing Mitzi-with-an-umbrella. My friend was smiling. He knew, I suppose, that I was a very appropriate category, but he wished me well nevertheless.

## OF MEN AND DOGS

If I were to tell you what a dog is feeling or thinking you would no doubt immediately think me a fool. You would know of course that a dog has a brain and therefore must use it in some way, that is, "think," But whether or not a dog can "feel" you would be far less certain of. (A sentimental dog, for example, is ludicrous.) And certainly, even granting a dog both, that is thoughts and feelings, you would be reluctant to allow that I might share either. And yet why not? Who is to prove different? Why is it not conceivable that *one person* might understand a dog perfectly (or even to some degree), as another a monkey, or a lizard. Granted that reptilian understanding seems (but perhaps only seems) too deep a biological divide (divide, I am aware, being too absolute a term), such confabulation would appear implicit in numerous common expressions, as when we call someone a dirty dog, foxy, a weasel, or lion-hearted. Lions, of course, are all lion-hearted, as are all foxes foxy; but we probably do dogs a disservice to call them dirty. No dog is dirty because doggy. And to think of weasels as "weasely" is a slur. Weasels are the best of their kind, and lions are not impressed with one another.

Nevertheless we persist, and as foolishly anthropomorphic as it all seems, I would like to suggest that it might be possible for an individual to *know* dogs, sheep, or any other creature. And it is possible, I think, for a person to have, say, a *truly* porcine nature, just as it is demonstrable that monkeys, billy goats, and other mammals have enormous pheromonal interest in human females at certain times. We might further speculate that it is possible that some dogs may truly know other dogs (or even other creatures) and that some rare dogs have inklings (I go no further, lest I ruffle rabid humanists) of humanness. Certainly it is true that some rare humans have insight to the thoughts and feelings of other humans. Babies, for example, progressing as they do by touch, taste, and smell, probably know mothers extremely well. Children and pets, also, seem to go well together. Perhaps the ages have programmed all of us towards only very peculiar understandings, however much society unprograms us. I certainly would not question the man who spoke passionately of his knowledge of tomatoes, or spiders, or even (remote as it seems) buttons, for that matter. We are all at peculiar and extreme points of evolution, whatever gaps or continuities we conceive of it as having. The problem (or one problem) is that we do not as a rule cohabit easily with tomatoes or spiders or buttons. We tend, socially, to look for visual similarity and community approval. For those who do not, we have various unpleasant asides. Even the arachnologist who married a spidery woman (not really awry: see the sparkling webby hair, the playful longish legs!) would be laughed at, mocked (although not the spouse of the jolly bovine girl, anthropologist take note!), if not considered downright loony. But so what, you will say, what is the point, what of it? Well, I don't know. At the moment it has just struck me as arrogant to deny categorically any one person's understanding of, say, dogs' thoughts or feelings (or a particular dog's, if you prefer). One person's meat is another person's dog. Ha. I have had the experience of feeling my fellow humans have no understanding of *me* at all. By the same token, I have walked down the street and been certain a dog was looking at me with amusement, even "laughing" at me. Was I wrong? Do any fools talk to their dogs? In some cases, a man proposing or professing his love might as well be a moose as far as the lady is concerned. Indeed the moose would be more understandable. Except, of course, with that particular woman for whom he had *better be a moose*. For her, happiness is moosiness. You think, of course, I jest. I suppose I do. But without jest could we ever escape truth, or arrive at truth? I do think it is possible I go too far. Only so far down the evolutionary ladder is real understanding possible. To make the oyster yield its pearl with song requires an effort of *imagination*, and there of course I place no limits. Yet is the chimera of validation any firmer in one than the other? The secret of a famous male star of screen is undoubtedly, unbeknownst to his admirers, his slow, reptilian lids. Who can say what purities course our blood? Who can fathom our archeology of bone? Was a famous writer of our century wrong to have his hero wake up an insect? Increasingly in our century we seek darkness, we seek the cracks and crevices of our cities or the parchness of our blasted plains, and there suck on our glittery frustrations like so many crickets. Perhaps we have denied too much of our understanding and have thereby become alienated from our planet, existentially "strange." For me, the wolf-man and the slithery-she are not unwelcome at my tea. I am eager to scratch any skin for enlightenment. Society is without doubt invisibly crawling. Progress has come round the bend. As have I, you say? Stuff and nonsense? Bosh? No. Say Bosch instead. Look into your mirror. Flit in and then out your slicky tongue. Blink your liddy eyes. Put tiniest digit into nostril, smile, hear your brackish bray, and try to unscramble your thoughts. A new Cuvier is needed here, with a new methodology, a poet's gift. Let me tell you a story, a small one, an anecdote. Evening. A man in a suit proudly walks his large dog. The dog defiles the sidewalk. Another man just behind shoots the dog. The owner of the dog strangles the man with the gun. The dog survives but is crippled. His owner goes to jail. Society kills the dog out of compassion. No one cleans the mess. Two days later it is still covered with flies. Then it rains. (It always rains.) Where does that leave us? I'm not sure. I think of

## The Man in the Stretcher

them all, particularly the dog, whom I do not understand at all. Shot, crippled, euthanized—did he have any thoughts between wound and execution? Did anyone see his eyes? I don't know. I do not, as I say, understand dogs. My intuitions are more with cats; sometimes, I think, with small birds, like the long-billed marsh wren. I have walked down that street many times, looked at that spot where very particular histories converged, pondered. Why, for example, did not the man with the gun, whose profession was the care of feet, shoot the man with the dog as he was strangled? Why did he have a gun? I do not know him either. And the man in prison? He has behind him, in another country, a sorrowful history, I am told. Does he miss his dog? His English is not good. This is a simple tale. Someone must know about it, understand it, see its flow. It is not my particular evolution to do so, even though it is now a part of my history, which will converge elsewhere. But there are other things I do understand. Some day I may write about them.

# LYCANTHROPE

I am sure I am not the only person in the world with lycanthrope fantasies. I am not joking at all. I genuinely wish I had the power to turn my head into a wolf's head (some few times it has been a tiger's head). Then, for example, I would challenge people: "So, you do not think I can frighten you? Well, then, come into the corner with me." Then, my back to everyone else, I would turn my head into a wolf's head so that she would scream. And, if not, I would lean closer with my foul feral breath, as if to kiss her. The smell would touch off her most primitive fear, and then she would surely scream, frantically, and run back to tell the others that I was a wolf. But when I turned I would have no wolf head, only a small smile. And they would laugh at her, but no one would ask to go into the corner with me. And for the rest of the evening she (and the others too) would watch me cautiously. How happy I should be in my silence. My pleasure, I assure you, would be extreme. And of course you wonder why. I know only how vivid and pleasurable that fantasy is. And it is not always the same. Sometimes, for example, I sit on the subway with my wolf's head while those few who notice me stare hard and wonder whether indeed I am a wolf. Sometimes I give a bloodcurdling howl that petrifies the whole car and send them all home in confusion. My lycanthrope fantasies are related to my Indian rope trick fantasies. In these, I have an audience, usually my colleagues. I have previously announced my exhibition, "Indian Rope Tricks, Levitation, Other Feats of the Mystic East." Of course, they snicker, but they come anyway, if only to see me make a fool of myself. I usually begin my program with a small box about a foot square on a bare table. The announced time comes, and nothing happens. They become restless. They make a few jeering remarks. Then my voice speaks from the box. They are silent a moment, then laugh. How obvious. a microphone in the box. But I call one of them up to take off the lid, the one who has jeered the loudest. He does so, and inside he sees my head peering at him and speaking. He faints. Others come and drag him away, glancing into the box. Then whispers among the audience. Yes, yes, it's true. He's *in* the box! Then my voice. Utter silence. "Will anyone come and help me out?" I ask. No one responds. They are all afraid. They are holding their breaths, perhaps expecting the box to burst. Then, breaking the silence, I walk to the stage from the back of the audience, go up to the box, put the lid on, smash it with my fist (there is a horrible scream from within), turn, and speak: "Welcome to 'Indian Rope Tricks, Levitation, and Other Feats of the Mystic East.'" There are no snickers now.

Everything is in dead earnest. I go through my tricks. I hold my arms out and have four, five, even six men hang from them. They do not bend. I have men run against me and try to knock me over. They fall down bruised and dazed. I am like a rock. I cannot be moved. And so on. I usually end my show by throwing a rope up in the air. It remains there. I climb up, look out at them, laugh, snap my fingers, and disappear. The rope collapses. End of show. Consternation, confusion, fear. They get up uneasily and walk out. Some few go on the stage and look at the smashed box. It is covered with blood. When next they see me, they keep a fearful but respectful distance. They all sense I could kill them in an instant if I wished. When I speak, all ears listen. Women become passionately interested in me. I do not take advantage of my power. I speak little but with quiet authority. I in no way gloat or call attention to myself. I dress conservatively but well. I am polite. I insist on my rights. I have announced for a future date an anthropological program in the music of African and Australian nose flutes. I am confident it will be a success.

# KEEPING A LOG

One of the charms of stories of the sea is the awareness that a log is always kept. In this respect, ocean travel appears to encapsulate a certain truth, namely that reality is a matter of keeping a record. One consults one's charts, registers longitude and latitude, plots one's directions, takes note of tide and wind, and jots down daily events, especially those which rise above the ordinary. But the ordinary itself is like a sea, beneath which lives a multiplicity of fabulous life, some of which we occasionally see. One never knows, for example, when a broken button will burst the surface of things and astonish us, absolutely astonish us. Hence, in keeping a log we are certain to feel some hesitation over what to record. It is only natural. Geography and weather, of course, are relatively easy. We have maps and books, and instruments, the concretions of time, to guide us. But after these certitudes, all else retains an instability, a recalcitrance, even some hidden threat. For example, it is difficult, when we record some human eruption, to then backtrack and put down some *sotto voce* judgement passed at mealtime, or a peculiar squint of the eyes, as its first visible ripple. The logbook is there in all its consecutiveness. We cannot just slip it in without breaking the rules. That wish is another kind of literature entirely. Nevertheless, there is always the desire to contain within one's log the significant events of one's experience, not to appear too much the fool. And this desire promotes, as often as not, an acute observation, a reluctance to dismiss too quickly any event one encounters as perhaps trivial or unworthy. Yet one must make decisions, take risks, for a log is no bible or history. A life at sea is a busy one, and one must trim one's log, like one's sails, to the exigencies of that life. The best one can do, perhaps, is to take some pot shots at the ordinary and to hope for the best. In that fashion, one's log stands a reasonable chance of reflecting substance of character and depth of perception. One will not too easily come off the blind fool. *Some wisdom will adhere to one's person.* I have, let me confess, taken this insight to heart and adapted it to my own log of my life's journey, some recent excerpts of which follow:

    Tuesday, July 11. Squashed toad on the road. Which way was he (she?) going? In a way, incomprehensible to me. On either side of the road was half of the world, perhaps even of the universe. Were they so different? Perhaps the road did not exist for the toad. In any event, its business was unfinished. How does it matter? The road does exist for me. It existed for him who squashed the toad. Here, somehow, we bisect. I go on. The toad does not. He died somewhere I am not. I walk somewhere *he* is not. Why is there this road?

    Wednesday, July 12. Again on the road. Same toad. Flies now. Does this mean that yesterday, when there were none, that the toad was freshly killed? I choose not to kick it aside. Today I notice the toad's insides, exploded out. Were they not there yesterday? The road does not exist for the flies either. The toad does. The toad exists for me also, but only as a toad on this road. At what point will the flies be done with the toad? How long will the skin of the toad be observable? I look for the toad both coming and going. It has become a marker. But of what?

    Thursday, July 13. Rain. Did not walk. Read instead, and thought of the toad. Convinced if I walked far enough I would see more toads. But why should I? My book is about love and pain. What object squashed the toad? Was there deliberation? And if so, what does that mean? Or not mean?

    Friday, July 14. No rain, but cloudy and somewhat cool. Wind. The toad is gone, but not the flies. I look for remains but see nothing. My eyes cannot penetrate. What *can* my eyes penetrate? I am bored with my book. The toad would be alive had it not attempted to cross the road. Is it possible that I walk on my road as intently as the toad crossed it? I don't think so. Am I being crushed? Perhaps.

    Sunday, July 15. Groceries again. Two miles by car. The sun is out. Guests tomorrow. Sick child. I have taken up my book again. The toad is fading from my mind. Do love and pain also split the world? Must we cross love and pain?

Sunday, July 16. A horrible dream. I am swallowed by a toad. The toad is crushed. The flies come. Where am I? What rendezvous did I miss? Guests interested in birds. A large dinner at two. Then the road. Two Philadelphia vireos by the raspberries and a female ruby-throat hovering one foot from my head. I know the spot perfectly, even though no flies. Say nothing. Guests have never heard of my book. Anxious for them to be gone. Rental payment sent. Child better. Wish it would rain.

—. Stars unusually bright. When they are not, the road is invisible. But if I stumble, perhaps I do not fall.

Monday, July 17. Not a week I am looking forward to. Height of summer. There is a mouse in the kitchen. Why? Wife wants me to set a trap. And if the mouse is caught in the trap? In great literature love is usually tragic. In trivial books, the reverse. Earthquake in the far West. Many deaths. Have decided to set the trap but not bait it. The trap is the road. Playing fair. Will watch where I walk. Neck fragile. Guests left at 11:00 PM. Asleep by midnight.

# ROAD-KILL

I am thinking about road-kill. Where were they going, and why? The road doesn't exist for them. Their topography and geography lie beneath our maps and our minds. And so they lie crushed or lingering by the roadside, and we, above, move on, unknowing. Of course there is road-kill everywhere. My aunt Anna, reptilian to the core, sought warmth and sun, heedless always, until her body erupted and rotted. She died uncomprehending, cruelly thwarted from her hot destiny, to lie in a cold place. What was her species? Where was she going? What was the road she was blind to? There is road-kill everywhere. And we are all implicated. Whole nations are implicated, crushed on roads they thought did not, or should not, exist, following their hard destinies. I am myself always engaged in trying to discover the roads that will destroy me. Of course, I do not find them all, or find them easily. All species, like my species of one, are prone to blindness of the roads on which they will be sacrificed. Not all, of course. Some few skitter from one side to the other, heedless of their luck. They move on, live longer, leave something or other behind, and die, perhaps even on a further road. The landscape is littered with us, the living road-kill, for whom we find names, and reasons, giving us a mockery of life, a languishing by the roadside, this one a weasel, this a fat woodchuck, that a philanthropist of great wealth, and still another a would-be saviour of the world. My family is a long history of road-kill, too poor for names, for taxonomies, but eking out their various deaths nevertheless. My fabulous uncle Harry, who spent much of his adult life in a dank, dirt-floor cellar, poking his fist into spider holes, chopping wood, where was he going? And why? What was his species? What name the road on which he expired? History itself is a story of road-kill. I read today of entire nations dying—of war, of disease, of corruption and twisted loyalties. Have they denominated the roads they are so heedlessly crossing? I think not. Road-kill, alas, is fundamental and enduring. Our visions are finite. I call my Uncle Harry fabulous for no reason I understand. I liked knowing where he was likely to be, where he stood, so to speak, liked being with him, mostly in silence, fearful of his exploits. No one has ever chopped wood as he did. Unerringly, he split all his logs true. His Rubicons were hidden, and complex. I alone bear that knowledge, and perhaps, to some degree, that skill. One day he disappeared. The cellar was vastly empty. And although I descended to its darkness, having inherited his chores, it was always a frightening descent, my return to the light of higher regions always a reprieve. He was, of course, spoken of, but less and less, until finally a fabled message that he might have been buried far to the west of us, near some final road. Or was it beyond all roads? I like to think that he died with a smile on his face, as if he had pursued his destiny as far as he could, with perseverance and great good luck. But of course I don't know. For I never knew where he was going. And now he is extinct, except perhaps for me. And I have, as yet, no name, nothing to mark me. I remember one year he kept his head shaved, but we never knew until the very end, because he wore his hat the entire time. Where is the taxonomy for that? Who would allow it to be called fabulous, like the gyrations of a brilliant jungle bird to no purpose perceived? To be sure, we do, at last, that bird demarcate, for its plumage *is* brilliant, and we are enamored of the word exotic. But might there not be wheels passing over us, blood pouring from our mouths as we laugh in full edification? Perhaps we are all lying by some roadside, quivering toward a last breath, unknowing of our true condition, all horizons shut down, and words flying above us like so many birds to their inglorious deaths. But if so, I am also thinking of my fabulous Uncle Harry, who lives marvelously in a realm of mystery, unmarked and unremarked, totally free. And *I* am smiling, slowly stretching my fist toward an unknown destiny.

# FLY-SWAT

It sometimes happens that I pursue my studies out of doors, in the world of nature, so to speak. I do this even though the tranquillity of my surroundings contradicts the darkness of some of my thoughts. My situation is by a picnic table in a grove of black locust trees, which I myself have thinned (for they seed prodigally). I sit in a comfortable white plastic chair on a gently sloping terrain, and I face the vegetable garden and a small picturesque fire pond. I know that a rather large snapping turtle lives in the pond because last year I saw her lay eggs in an aged manure pile by that part of the garden where I plant my squashes. Overall, I find I am able to call forth my somber muse sufficiently, although I sometimes wonder whether I am more cheerful than I ought to be. I tend, for example, to look more benignly on the fat woodchucks whose dens are under the tall grasses surrounding the garden. The insects, I admit, bother me to a certain degree, and I do not like waving my arms or hat about to discourage them. My wife, no doubt seeing me flail about, has thoughtfully provided me with an excellent fly-swatter, laying it quietly across my dictionary. Now, of course, from one perspective this is silly, even laughable. What does it mean to kill one fly or spider or ant? Or even ten? Their realm is large, and others will come to replace them. I learned this years ago when I borrowed a neighboring farmer's gun to shoot at depredating woodchucks near our garden. "Why do you bother?" he finally said to me. "Do you not think others will come to replace them?" I realized he was right, that woodchucks had their own sense of territory, in which I was a negligible factor; and since then, whenever we see a woodchuck near or in the garden, my wife simply runs out, yelling, "Go 'way! Go 'way!" Sometimes they do, and sometimes they don't. We live on a kind of share plan, but never a predictable one. I have gone so far as to plant two rows of diversionary beans (from old seeds). My wife's charges give me considerable amusement, and perhaps that is why she provided me with a fly-swatter—to give her some amusement back. Of course, I could simply go indoors, where there are fewer insects, but I have seen too many paintings and read too much poetry to leave the field in defeat. Although nature does not *belong* to me, I persist in feeling that I have some place in it, albeit a meditative and contemplative one. I have, in fact, swatted several irksome creatures with the swatter, utterly squashing them, laughing at myself at the same time for my folly. No doubt my wife is waiting for me to cry out, "Go 'way! Go 'way!" which is coming to have a classic ring. So far I have not. But just recently I hit upon a new stratagem, and, for all

I know, some inadvertent biological, or other, fact. Swinging very awkwardly one day—for who can predict the gyrations of insects—I disabled but did not kill a winged creature. I was about to deliver the *coup de grace* when something forestalled my hand. I realized the creature was buzzing, that this buzzing was very a possibly a distress call warning others of its kind to keep away, much as the moans of a semi-executed prisoner might serve as a similar warning. The thought enchanted me, and I thereafter adjusted my strokes to wound but not to kill (surely a stroke of applied intellect), and the picnic table each day became littered with the dying of various species, creating a symphony of distress, much of which I was certain I could not hear, despite its presumed efficacy. There are, of course, still problematics to my system. For example, the distress calls themselves (if indeed they are such), provide their own disturbance. Then there are what I interpret as their frantic movements, similar to those of insects on fly-paper. My eye keeps wandering to their funereal ballet. *They are going nowhere!* There is also the matter of the number of species in the grove. (And what, exactly is a *grove*?) I cannot accept that the distress calls of one species are effective with the members of another species, as if we might share a universal distress. So how many dismembered and mutilated species must I accumulate to insulate myself effectively? That knowledge would entail considerable study of my natural environment. (Ah. So much for *Ephemerida*. Now on to *Plectophora*.) I do not have the time, nor, I'm afraid, the talent or training. The peonies are in full glorious bloom, and the birds—cowbirds, purple finches, hummingbirds, chickadees, goldfinches—are busy at their different feeders. An occasional hairy woodpecker pecks beneath the locust barks. They are no problem, not yet anyway. But, increasingly, I have the feeling that somehow problems are accumulating and will continue to do so, beyond anything already mentioned. For example:

1. When I have finished my morning's work, what should I do with my menagerie? Do I summarily execute them? Do I sweep them off the table to other destinies, e.g., food for other creatures? Do I simply leave them and let their reverberations permeate the air? Is some ritual required?

2. I know enough about biology to know there are always sports, mutants that do not correspond to proper laws. Thus, within each species, there will always be some who do not respond to distress signals. What is their potential for annoyance? What would be their jarring music were they among the mutilated?

3. The woodchucks that eat my vegetables—what if I left them similarly disabled around the garden? Would their distress calls keep others away? Would they be silent at night? Should I feed and water them? What might visitors think? How far does

this go?

4. Is there perhaps an arrangement of clothing that would integrate me perfectly in my grove? This, I realize, is a matter of some scope. See, for example, the great jungle explorers. Or consider the quaint notion of camouflage (I rather *like* the idea of myself as a *camoufleur*). There is, of course, also the notion of total *protection*, but this is another discourse.

5. Did the snapping turtle lay her eggs again this year in our garden? If not, why not? Should we have replaced the manure pile?

6. I speak of a *symphony* of distress. Is that the proper word? Do I need also to study musicology? What else do I need to study?

7. My wife has said nothing about the dying insects on the picnic table. Why not? Does she still find my predicament amusing? *Is* it amusing?

8. When the snapping turtle pulls down a duck, is there a cry of distress?

9. Is it possible that I myself have been (am) mutilated and my life a series of cries of distress. Am I, somehow, being *pulled down, swept off*? Is there a sociology, a philosophy, or a theology to be built on this?

10. The day that something forestalled my *coup de*

*grac*e upon the injured insect—what was that something? What might it mean if I labeled it God?

11. Who or what (if anything) *really* put the fly-swatter in my hand? How many other things have come to hand in that manner? And with what consequences?

12. *classic ring*—what exactly do I mean by attributing it to the cry "Go 'way!'"? Our forays into "nature" seem at least equally to be balanced by some wish for it simply to disappear. How close do, or can, we really get to our woodchucks? On the other hand, what would the space of our garden be like without them? Also, this drama, in a certain sense, is also played out *within* ourselves. There is surely a *human* nature that intersects somewhere with a *woodchuck* nature. But where? Answers here are difficult, even merely to contemplate.

13. *The fly-swatter on my dictionary.* Aside from my wife's sly humor, the image does resonate with heraldic force. I realize that many gestures in life have similar resonance, if only we could see it. I have resolved to improve my vision. For example, I suddenly realize that our "unpredictable share plan" with the woodchucks might just be such a gestural moment. But at the same time that this excites me it also makes me feel insane. How, for example, could I explain to anyone a recurring manure pile for turtle eggs? Or litanies for dying insects?

14. Should I try "arranging" the components of my "symphony"? Am I possibly a *composer* of some sort? A *compositeur*?

15. I say that nature does not belong to me. But do *I* belong to it? If so, why do I not feel it? If not, to what *do* I belong? Am I an interloper in the universe?

16. Swinging my swatter awkwardly—I realize that I can never swing my swatter with the precision that the hangman fits his noose and releases the trap door. In nature I am a failed acrobat. Elsewhere I can achieve perfection.

17. The disturbance of the distress calls of dying insects—what is the nature of that disturbance? Do I possibly feel (in addition to the noise) some atavistic *sympathy*? I'm afraid I repeat myself (but what else can I do?)

18. Finally, I refer above to my morning's work. The question can be asked, what, exactly, *is* my morning's work? Do my tabulations occupy me too much? I feel that I might, but only just, be on the verge of a new arrangement with life. This will cause problems.

I'm afraid my lucubrations have taken a metaphysical turn. Perhaps all things eventually take on a metaphysical turn. But what, then, does that mean? Is it possible that a simple fly-swatter can be an instrument of fate? I realize that I have not been forthcoming about the nature of my sometimes dark thoughts before the fly-swatter. They do not seem relevant here. Perhaps they are not relevant at all. Suffice it to say that they are based on considerable reading, reflection, and observation. They are both empirically and analytically informed. They will undoubtedly make their appearance at a later time, when I am unstuck from my present obsessions.

# THE DREAM OF WRITING IN ARABIC SCRIPT

The dream of writing in Arabic script is not entirely farfetched. One can always, for example, *study* Arabic script, study Arabic, in fact. But that is not the same as the *dream* of writing in Arabic script. The dream of writing in Arabic script is a dream of grace and otherness, a sudden advent to a perfumed garden surrounded by a wall. And what is in that garden? Women, of course, voluptuous and clad for the heat, perhaps lolling men talking of philosophy, eating tropical fruits. Moving waters also, and enough low-lying trees for shade. But there seems to be no egress, no curlicued gate leading to crowds and hot streets where business is transacted. Nor are there insects, or animals, and I find this odd. If I were to go there, I could not get out. Unless, of course, I *studied* Arabic script. Then I could explore the dusty streets and mingle with the crowds. Could I get back to the garden? That is not certain. The streets wind and twist. Where they go is not clear. Perhaps they do not go anywhere. It is difficult to rush, or to take long strides. I am, of course, overwhelmed there by smells—urine and dung, rotting food, body odors, food preparations, smoke, blood. Here the women are amply covered, except for the eyes, the utterances are loud and harsh, no one is looking at me but I am watched, observed. *Studying* Arabic script is difficult. One doesn't get back to the garden easily, perhaps not at all. It seems there might be two Arabic scripts, maybe more. In my dream I write script beautifully and quickly. It flows. It is rich, direct, and strong, with no hesitations. But no one can read it. "How beautiful!" they might say, "but what does it mean?" If I point to the beautiful women or the fountain, they look blank. They might even laugh. "What you need," they say, "is a snake or two in your garden." "But what would they eat?" I ask. And they laugh again. "That is the question," they say, "is it not? — What do snakes eat?" I have never thought about that. "But are there not snakes in the village, in the town?" I ask. "Not many," they say. "They are dangerous. We kill them." We are silent a long time. I am thinking about snakes in the garden. What they are thinking I do not know. Finally, I say, "If there were snakes in the garden, the women would charm them and let them wind around them. The men would watch and laugh. But they would not get up. They will never get up. Perhaps the snakes would eat pomegranate. I'm not sure." In my dream I speak to the sitting men in Arabic, but the sounds are gibberish. No one seems to mind. One of the women even smiles at me. How gorgeous and lush is her body, how tempting, even with snakes coiled around her. However, I do not attempt to approach her, to go near to her. Somehow I sense that it is forbidden. These are not the snakes that were recommended for my garden, for my dream of writing in Arabic script. I look about me, at first covertly, then desperately, for a path that will lead to a gate. I want to get out. I do not yet know that there is no gate, there is no right path. There is only here, forever. To find a gate I must awaken from my dream and begin studying Arabic script, frantically even. And then, slowly, the smell of camel, maybe goat, will lead me into a street, and then another, and another, until I am lost. There will be dust in my nose and throat. My eyes will blur with tears. And when I am truly lost, someone, perhaps, will look at me very directly, a man, of course. Out of my dry throat I will utter a sound, a croak. Is it Arabic? The man will nod and move on. At this point I will have lost the garden. At this point, the first curlicues of Arabic script will have formed in my mind and I will seek a place to write them. But even then, at that point, I will wonder, ask myself, "Is this another dream of writing Arabic script? Is this another in a series of dreams of writing in Arabic script? At that very moment, a snake will bite me.

# TRAVEL GUIDE

There is obviously a need for new travel guides. Those in existence tell us nothing and guide us nowhere, just as our dictionaries do not define anything. That we are overjoyed upon returning from journeys so predicated is proof only of profound asininity, of non- or deferred existence. True also of those who bask in our asinine glow, promising to imitate us with all possible dispatch. Lemmings all, to the sea! In mitigation, let it be said that many decent enough men and women feed their children and pay the rent, foster the common weal and promote suitable metaphysics pandering these inanities—genuine Guatemalan handicrafts for breakfast, so to speak, camels munching in the moonlight for lunch, and thuggee legend for dinner.

But where, for example, is the guide for a certain nameless Central American village of no distinction, where one steaming morning in June of 199–, in a garbage-littered and unpaved street, the dogs too hot already to forage but not several small pigs and a few scrawny chickens, a certain Maria Ribajo, aged nine and barefoot, in a faded but newly washed blue dress already too small for her, dropped, and then, after quickly looking up and down the street, picked up a small loaf of bread, brushed off the dust, and returned, with some trepidation, to her anxious mother? Two dogs look up, but only for a moment. Nothing significant had occurred in their universe. Maria gone, the buzzing of the flies was heard above the snortling of the pigs. The sun, as always, beat down without mercy. Later that day several throats would be cut and a slogan written on a wall, which, translated, said, "BE THE PEOPLE!"

Two miles away, two tourists sipped fruit juices and were blinded by the floral beauty of what they saw. One was named Helen and the other Dora. They were, unknowingly, in love with the same man, who was to join them for further journeying. One of them would sleep with him; the other would come down with dysentery and, some time later, die. By then she would have been abandoned by the other two and, idly, listlessly, leafing through her travel guide, she would discover that she was in the wrong place at the wrong time. Outside her room, two girls who cleaned, or seemed to, would be whispering conspiratorially, but the woman in bed would not know about what because she did not know the language. She had never known the language. She had, indeed, no use for that language or any other.

Maria's mother had nine children by four men, one of them a husband, who had long since left and was possibly dead or a revolutionary or both. She was fat and tired, nearly toothless, and looked far older than her age, which was thirty-eight. Seven of her children were dead. The one, other than Maria, who was alive had wandered off before he was ten. He also was possibly a revolutionary. The bread had to last two days and then they would see what would come next.

    The woman in the bed dreamed one night of a Latin lover, but it was a woman. The dream troubled her. Her luggage was stolen after her third day in bed. Only her underclothing and bed clothes were left, as if a sign of destiny. She had paid in advance and so had some time in which to die. In a land of so much fruit juice it never occurred to her that she might be dehydrated. The young women who seemed to clean did not appear to mind her filth. They even giggled as they worked, and wore flowers in their hair. Their rumps were well filled and both had beautiful teeth. The woman in the bed looked forward to their visits. Because there was a telephone, she was able to get still more money, and she thought she would, when she was well, buy one of the girls a present, a bright dress perhaps, or sandals.

    Maria's mother had no special man in her life, but rather several casual men. They were fat also. One of them regularly made suggestions to Maria, which she repeated to her mother. Her mother said nothing. She neither smiled nor looked angry. She just stared at Maria, who felt uncomfortable and went outside to watch the dogs. For the first time she wondered when they ate, when, in fact, they did anything. They did not seem bothered by the flies on them. They seemed to sleep all the time. She had never wanted one as a pet. Her mother puzzled her. She, Maria, had begun menstruating several months earlier. She wondered who her father was and where he had gone. Two days earlier she had seen a man in a ditch. He was naked, and bad things had been done to him. His teeth seemed very large. There were some women in the ditch also. She wished she had some roasted iguana to eat.

 The woman in the bed, Dora, soon began to think that time in Central America was different, that it did not matter much what she wore or whether she was in bed or out of bed. Under the hum of the insects, everything seemed the same. She sipped, ate, went weakly to the latrine for one thing or another, and slept at odd times, contemplating the sweat on her body for long intervals. It was something of a strange luxury. It occurred to her that she might be beautiful, sexually alluring, but the thought did not excite her. When the young women came in, she left her breasts exposed, but they did not seem to notice. One day, the one she liked better revealed that she was trying to learn English. "I want," she said, "learn better the English. I want be movie star. I want fuck rich man." Where had she learned such English, the woman wondered. Another day, the young woman, a girl, really, came in and fondled Dora's breast. "I yam," she said proudly,

"Miss Lollapalooza Big Ass." Then she laughed raucously, giving Dora's nipple a hard tweak as she left. All this gave the woman in the bed much to think about.

Maria's mother meanwhile began to have difficulty walking. One leg became swollen and discolored, as if she had been bitten by a poisonous creature. A local man who was thought to know something about medical practice said it would have to come off, implying that he would be willing to do the job. The fat men began to stay away because of the smell, and Maria had to attend to her mother's every need. Her faded blue dress got dirty. The dogs began to sleep closer to the hut. Occasionally one fat man or another would leave food. Maria's mother was determined to keep her leg. With two legs, a lot was possible.

Both women died the same day. The morning of the day Dora died, her young woman came in and seemed to want money for a plane ticket. It was considerably more than sandals or a dress, Dora thought. As far as she knew, the movie star Carmen Miranda had worn big hats but had no big ass, to speak of. Suddenly she laughed, feeling pleasantly at risk on the verge of some new knowledge or experience. Perhaps things had changed, she thought. Perhaps her young woman *would* become a movie star. She reread the postcard she had received from Helen the day before. Helen was ecstatically happy, but she knew such passion could not last. The postcard featured a lagoon. Two minutes before Maria's mother died, she gave Maria another of her hard looks and asked, "You know how to do it? Do you know how to do it?" It had been years, she thought, since she had cried. What was the point? Maria stared at her mother a long time before she realized her mother was dead. She did not cry either, then or later.

[Addenda. There are several points in the narration above which might, for some, need clarification. They are listed in no taxonomic order:
1. Maria's mother—what was her name?
2. Maria's mother—what was the disease that afflicted her leg?
3. Maria's mother—why did so many of her children die, and of what?
4. Maria's mother—was she religious? If not, was there any thing else that sustained her?
5. The lagoon in the postcard sent by Dora's friend—was it the site where she was conducting her affair? That is, was it something she actually saw? Or was it just something she thought suitable to represent where she was and what she was engaged in? What, exactly, was she engaged in? Did the man send his regards? Should we know more about him?
6. The bread Maria dropped—who had baked it and how much had it cost? Why could not her mother bake bread?
7. Maria's mother—what are things she thought possible with two legs that were not possible with one leg, that is, other than walking, jumping, etc.?
8. The man who said the leg of Maria's mother would have to come off—had he ever cut off a leg (or anything else) before? From what did he derive his confidence? What else could he do?

9. The two girls who cleaned Dora's room—what were *their* names? Why did Dora prefer one to the other? Why did the one she preferred fondle her breast and pinch her nipple? Was it simply a good-natured act, a service like changing the linens, or a calculated act with mercenary intent? If the last, what else might she have done? Did she think Dora a lesbian, and did it matter? Was Dora, in fact, a lesbian—or something else? And if so, whatever it was, how much did it owe to *where* she was? Where, in fact, was she?
10. What did the girls whisper and giggle about? Did they know about the slit throats and mutilated men and women in ditches? If so, did they care? Why or why not?
11. Was Maria's mother political? Did one eat better if one was political? Sleep better?
12. Who were the fat men who came to Maria's mother, and what were their family situations?
13. How well did Maria understand the word "it" in her mother's final words? How soon after her mother's death did she, in fact, do "it," whether she had understood or not, and with whom? Did the fat men go to the funeral? Did anybody go?
14. The husband of Maria's mother—what cause was he fighting (or had he died) for? Was Maria's only living brother *with* him, fighting or dying for the same cause? Why had the boy's father left Maria's mother? What was *his* name?
15. How old were Dora and Helen? What did they do in life? What did they not do in life?
16. How did Dora know about the size of Carmen Miranda's ass, and what, if anything, should be inferred from that?
17. Were the fat men political? Was the man Maria saw in the ditch fat? How old were the fat men? How old were the people in the ditch?

18. How much did Maria understand about the world? Did she love her mother? Or was love beside the point? Might she have become like the girls who attended Dora? Or was that out of the question, and if so, why?
19. Why does not Dora seem angry about Helen's running off with the man she thought she loved?
20. What country does Dora die in, and how long had she been there? (cf.#9).
21. From whom, in fact, had the young girl who wanted to be a movie star learned her pidgin English? And how did "Lollapalooza" come to be featured in it?
22. What is the meaning of Dora's dream? Is it possible her entire journey is a dream?…If so, when and where will she wake up?
23. When Maria went out for bread, why was her mother anxious?
24. What would have been "significant" in the eyes of the sleeping dogs of Maria's village?
25. What does it mean that Dora had no interest in the local language or, in fact, any language? Does this include her own language? What *is* her language? Where, in fact, is she from and what is she doing in Maria's village, whether by design or accident? While contemplating the sweat on her body for long intervals, is she possibly on the verge of learning another language? Why do the insects not bother her?
26. Had Maria's mother, in fact, been bitten by a poisonous creature? If so, what was it? Are there jungles nearby? Who, or what, lives in them?
27. Did Maria have all her teeth? Was she fat? Thin? Was she shapely in back? How much longer did she wear her faded blue dress, and what finally happened to it? How much does she resemble her mother?

28. Would the dogs have eaten Maria's mother's rotten leg, had they the opportunity? Were they really as asleep as they seemed to Maria?
29. Who stole Dora's luggage and most of her clothing, and what did he/she/they know? Were there any books in the luggage?
30. In what sense can Dora be said to have been abandoned by Helen and her lover? Did *she* feel abandoned?
31. In what sense can *anyone* ever be said to be in the wrong place at the wrong time? In that sense, is Dora any different from Maria's mother? Or the dogs? Or the flies? Is "displacement" a word or a reality? Did Carmen Miranda, never from Central America, with a basket of tropical fruit on her head, singing and dancing her Latin best for Hollywood moguls, feel displaced? If not, where was she? Where is anybody?
32. The phrase "and so had time in which to die"—do not we all have some time in which to die, and a language, and a place in which to do it?
33. Is it possible that Maria watched the dogs in the same way that the woman in the bed contemplated her sweat? Or her mother watched *her*? What about the chickens and the pigs? What about the flies? Is it possible that Maria will become a philosopher? Was her mother a philosopher? Were the fat men philosophers? Could this be a history of the world?
34. What did the fruit on Carmen Miranda's head mean? Is it possible that Helen and Dora were looking for fruit to put on their heads? It is written that Carmen Miranda, although shrewd in the ways of the world, came to a sad end. Why? Was she buried with fruit on her head? Did *she*, in the end, become a philosopher? Do philosophers have baskets of fruit on their heads?

35. Why does not Maria seem to have playmates? Has Maria, in fact, ever played? Are there puppies in the village?
36. What is a dog universe? What is an ant universe? Is there a rock universe? (Is there a rotten leg universe).
37. What is the taste of roasted iguana?
38. Is there a connection among teeth, buttocks, legs, and dogs? What other connections might there be? What is a connection?
39. There is something that matters about Maria's dropping of the bread, but what is it? Why, really, does she look up and down the street? How does one characterize that moment of silence, of stillness?
40. Why did not the thought that she might be sexually alluring excite the woman in the bed? *Was* she, in fact, sexually alluring?
41. Is her name more Dora or The Woman in the Bed?
42. Maria's mother—was she a whore?—Did Maria become a whore? If so, is that what she thought she was? On whatever level, what does the fly on the back of a sleeping dog in a Central American village think it is?
43. Did Maria remain in her mother's hut? How was it furnished?
44. What is it like to have your throat cut? What is it like to have your leg cut off by a peasant? What is it like to have your testicles stuffed in your mouth? What is it like to have a knife where a penis might be? These are difficult questions to answer second-hand. All questions are difficult to answer second-hand.

These addenda are written for clarification. In some cases, they might raise still other questions, other matters. That cannot be avoided. Unfortunately, there is not the space in which to follow through completely.]

Nine days. $18,249,999,380.00, travel not included. 40% off, June-August. Off-beat and unspoiled. Deposit required.

# FLÂNEUR

I'm not sure when I first noticed that the birds had stopped singing. But they had. Perhaps, I thought, it was a premonition of early frost. Perhaps something else. At first, it seemed a salutary silence, part of a larger one I had been seeking, and I rather enjoyed it. But gradually it began to lose its charm. The birds went about their business, but it was a dumb show. Nature had created a silent drama, and I felt implicated. What had happened? What was the meaning of birds that made no sound? I found myself, finally, poised for their merest twitter. But it did not come. I wondered whether I myself had somehow created the silence, had somehow gone too far in my retreat from the noises of the world. And immediately I wondered about those other noises, too. Had they also gone? I didn't really want to think about it, and I comforted myself with the idea that I could, whenever I wished, *will* all noise back into being. And there I let the matter rest.

    Several days later, the silence at the back of my mind, I remembered a friend, an acquaintance, with whom I had consorted for a time, years earlier. I never knew what really threw us together, or why I thought of him now. We had little in common. And we talked less. Mostly we walked about our city, stopping here and there, silently agreeing that we could not be heard above the manifold noises of the city, even had we been inspired to speak. But sometimes we hit upon a crooked street or square, occasionally a small park inhabited by old people or derelicts, even a bench, where silence was suddenly palpable. The derelicts, having found their own silence, ignored us, but the old people stared, as if we had been put there for their grotesque entertainment. And perhaps we had been. For we did feel, because of the silence, impelled to speak at last. But we spoke softly, so they would not really hear us. In the streets and squares, the buildings themselves seemed to stare, even lean, at us, and we spoke softly there, too, so they should not hear, so their stones and bricks would retain no story, no stain. My acquaintance's name was Fred, which surprised me, because I had expected it to be something like Wolfgang or Fritz. Why, I'm not sure. Perhaps because his clothes fit him so loosely. And because I fancied that he spoke with a slight accent. But, on reflection years later, I decided it was not an accent but rather that his voice was rusty, from lack of proper use. Something like a hinge on an old garden's gate. He, too, lived in a silence.

    I'm pretty sure I had met Fred in a bookstore. We had started talking in a dusty alcove about one book or another. I know it must have been a specific book, but I have forgotten what it was. And that bothers me, because it was a beginning, and beginnings matter. At any rate, one thing led to another, and we left to have coffee in a nearby cafe. That became the first of many encounters and walks, all of which I found soothing, even exciting, although nothing much ever happened. Or so I thought. I looked forward, you might say, to our boredom and a certain repetition. I'm not sure what Fred did for a living, what he had to do to pay his rent and put food on the table, as we all must, but I think he was a very minor official somewhere, a handler of meaningless paper. He had once, I think, elsewhere, been married, but now lived alone in cramped quarters with his many books, mementos, and other oddities, documents perhaps. I was never invited there. Perhaps he was ashamed. Or tired. Perhaps he no longer entertained. But he clearly enjoyed my company, for reasons I could never fully understand. For I was, of the two of us, the more outgoing, the more forward-looking. I was the one more eager to get on with things. For Fred, everything seemed already to have happened, although what those things were I never found out. At any rate, we did, as I say, talk a bit in our quiet streets, our little squares and hidden parks. But I'm at a loss to recall much of what we talked about. I know he was fond of music, of Chopin, in particular. Did that mean he was Polish? Or perhaps a romantic? The latter did not seem likely. Aside from the unknown book that had introduced us, our literary tastes were quite different. Whereas I aimed at inclusion and coherence, he seemed quite scattered and incoherent. One week he would be absorbed with Bedouins in some remote pocket of the globe and talk with great relish about their bitter coffee on cold desert mornings. Another week it would be some treatise on the behavior of ants, which charmed him no end. Where was the connection? How did he get from one week to the next, so to speak? The answer, in a word, was that he didn't. Weeks did not exist for him anymore. Nor connections. In one of our talking interludes he spoke a lot about connections, even grammatical ones, and laughed a lot, which was rare. Coordination, for example, seemed a cosmic joke to him. Several times he muttered to me, "You poor boy. You poor dear boy." I suppose I should have been insulted, but the truth is I didn't know what he was talking about. Ponder the "and," indeed. But I indulged him. I knew he was getting at something, whether I knew what it was or not. And I liked him. Partly, of course, because he seemed to like me. And that in part was because I, like him, was an aimless stroller of the city, a seeker of refuge, a refugee from noise. I suppose, to get into his drift of things, we were sinking deeply into some sort of endless subordination, footnotes without end. The only other conversation I recall clearly, and only the end of it, at that, was the one that concluded with a question. After an hour of aimless but not uninteresting talk, he turned to me and asked, "Have you noticed that the silence is growing, that we are slowly but surely becoming *engulfed* by it?" This struck me as indeed strange, for when he asked his question, we were not in one of our secluded havens from noise but rather on a main thoroughfare, crowded with bustling, well fed, purposeful people, and I could barely hear him. "Hardly," I replied, and laughed. He joined me in my laughter, for he was not without a sense of humor.

    Shortly after that, again for reasons I cannot remember or perhaps never knew, we ceased to see each other. Our walks, our conversations terminated, and I moved on in life, as we say. I lost track of our quiet streets and squares and parks. Perhaps they have been razed and rebuilt, with new monuments, celebrating new men and women, new ideas, like consanguinity. Perhaps he retired on a small pension and went to warmer climes. I don't know. I moved on, as I have already said. Remarkably, some time later I met a youngish man who claimed to be his son. He was no Wolfgang either. He said that he had last seen his father when he, the son, was on the threshold of manhood. His mother had died unpleasantly somewhat earlier. He said that he, the father, was an odd and silly bugger. Although that was close to what I myself had often thought, I confess that I was angry. In fact, I nearly struck him for the twit he was. I realize now that Fred was not an odd and silly bugger at all, but an extraordinary man who taught me a great many things, although I could not enumerate or describe them. Nor do I think that Fred was his real name, but rather a strange accommodation he had decided upon, perhaps even an obscure joke. The son also implied that my friend had not retired and moved to warmer climes, but that he had ended his own life, very quietly, and left no note of explanation. I felt devastated, bereft, empty, on the point of real tears, but almost as quickly I wondered what had happened to the books he so carefully annotated, his archive, for he was a great collector and recorder of oddities. As for the son, although I am sorry for him, I do not, on reflection, really believe him. Fred had gone to another place, to be sure, a deeper and darker place, but it was not the place of self-inflicted death. He had gone beyond that, somewhere he could quietly finish his commentaries before his natural end.

    And now, as I watch my silent birds, a nature gone dead, I have a sudden inspiration, the first I have had in a very long time, to verify whether I myself might indeed have created the silence around me and to leave my retreat for the city we once trod, our city, and there, amidst the noises that surely still exist, to search out a silent square, a hidden park, a bench even, to see what traces I might find, whom I might meet, to stare intensely, to listen, to discover some truth, inadequate as it might be, perhaps even to *remember*, to recover the book that had begun our adventures. And others. For surely Fred's final library must exist somewhere, dusty perhaps, in a silence of its own, waiting. And I suddenly realize, at this very moment, that it is what I truly yearn for, that it is all I yearn for, and that it is—I do see that now—my only salvation.

# THE WAR OF THE FOOTNOTISTS AND ENDNOTISTS

It has occurred to me that the world might easily be divided into footnotists and endnotists. I, of course, count myself among the former. My wife, on the other hand, is an endnotist. I am trying in my subtle way to convert her. But no matter how much progress I might seem to make, the conflict arises ever anew in a thousand small ways—coffee cups, so to speak, the view from the window. I like to footnote as I go along in life. I have no confidence in waiting to the end to wrap everything up. That kind of closure is too much like death. And in peeking ahead, in the shuffling back and forth, I lose the text, I forget what I am reading. I like instead the immediate dropping into the footnote. Indeed, for me the footnote is a part of my text, especially inasmuch as I find that just about everything requires a footnote. I have thought about the subject a good deal and have formulated a few working principles, which I shall state as briefly as possible:

1. Most things in life require footnotes.
2. Footnotes are always text also.

3. All footnotes require their own footnotes, etc.
4. Thus all footnotes run off the page and are never concluded. That is, all footnotes fail.
5. All footnotes change the text they are footnotes to. Thus, as per #3 and #4, no text is ever finished either.
6. Footnotes eventually swallow "text." That is, "text" is a delusion.

Now of course in any text there are physical and metaphysical limits. Life in that way is imperfect. I accept that. For example, when a particular primary footnote is not concluded on its page I feel a particular thrill in turning the page because it adumbrates a certain disarray, an ill-fittingness in life: there is always more, but I shall never know all of it. But this turning of the page (and then of course returning to the text before) is not like the turning to and from endnotes. Endnotes conclude and seal off. Endnotes have no subsequent endnotes to themselves. Their containment is perfect. So in turning to them we seek an assurance and confirmation rather than an extension of doubt and uncertainty. People therefore are far more likely to argue about footnotes than endnotes. Perhaps a few things might be said about endnotes:

1. It is increasingly the nature of endnotes to precede text. That is, text is there, but irrelevant.

2. Endnotes are perfect.
3. All texts to endnotes are therefore also perfect.
4. Death is always beautiful and on time.

I think everyone more or less begins life as an endnotist, at a mother's breast. A mother and a father are the endnotes children frequently turn to. Life probably needs endnotes to get us through some difficult years. But in time, for most children, parents become footnotes, and footnotes of footnotes, etc. The shape of the world changes. They digress. There is less turning to the end and more drowning into the page they are reading. Perhaps it would be good here to say that footnotes have until recently been monumentally misunderstood. It has long been presumed that footnotes clarify. They do not. They complicate, lead only to the labyrinth or to the abyss. The shifting of them to the end of a text has not been a mere spatial change but an inevitable substantive change. A corrective. To speak of efficiency in comprehension, in printing, publishing, etc., is disingenuous. We have advanced, not regressed, technically: footnotes, if anything, should be less of a problem. The advent of endnotes has made it quite clear (to me, at any rate) that footnotes have never been part of the solution to any problem but rather a deepening of the problem. They are and have been murky waters. Hence the flight from them. Not so with me. I am no child of light. I revel in the delirium of footnotes and am scornful of the tranquility of endnotes. Endnotes, indeed. I do not wish to be buried before my time. So what about my wife, my coffee cup, and so on? Well, to be brief but not clear, I have a favorite cup for my coffee. I also have a favorite soup bowl and a thousand other oddities of character. I could, for example, talk at great length about a dead Aunt Netti. Let me stick with my cup. Quite simply, the other morning my wife poured me coffee in the wrong cup. It wasn't that my favorite cup was unavailable or that my wife was being mischievous or worse. One cup just happened to be more accessible than the other (I don't stop to talk about "accessible.") And there is no doubt that I could have drunk my coffee from that cup. Indeed, I have, entirely on my own, done so. But at that place at that time I would not have enjoyed it as much. So I simply poured from one cup to another. Our civilization has several names for such an act. My wife laughed. Sitting on a sheaf of endnotes she said, "What's the difference? It's the same coffee, isn't it? The same kind of cup?" The questions were difficult to answer. I mean, of course, the answer to both questions was no. No, it was not the same coffee, any more than you can cross the same river twice. And no, it was not the same kind of cup. But how, sinking into my footnotes, could I explain? For example,

    1.    There was only one cup and it was one of a kind, regardless of how much it looked and felt like

another.
2. The cup had a history too numerous to detail, some of it unknown to me but nevertheless felt.
3. The coffee was not the same. The coffee took its being from where it was. And not all of its being was material.
4. It mattered a great deal to me that a) she had poured the coffee in the wrong cup and b) she thought my "predicament" funny. Of course, my "predicament" was life itself. Equally, many would think me a fool. I could have chosen to illustrate with a more serious example, maybe brain surgery—but what, really is "more serious"? Better I should immediately be thought a fool and avoid unnecessary talk. There is never any fooling an endnotist. To sum up, I am a footnotist, unreconstructed and seriously on the loose. And unless they cage me, as indeed they are trying to do, I shall wreak chaos on this world.

Additional Commentary:

1. An obvious question is what things in life, then, do not require footnotes? The only thing that comes

immediately to mind is death, and I have doubts about even that.

2. It goes without saying that a true endnotist has no need of footnotes. But it can sometimes be observed that an endnotist will resort, in the place itself, to an asterisk. Dare I suggest that this is dangerous ground and that an asterisk might itself have an asterisk?

3. Bibliographies are always disguised endnotes. The same is true of tables of contents.

4. Clearly the shift from footnotes to endnotes is paradigmatic. Footnotists are therefore a threat and should probably be shot. Advocates of particularity have no future.

5. Can a footnotist find happiness with an endnotist? Yes, but only if he or she footnotes happiness. Can an endnotist find happiness with a footnotist? Hard to say.

# MY NEW LIBRARY

It has occurred to me only recently how foundational the idea of a library is. That is because I am planning what will probably be my final move in life, and I want my new dwelling to have a library. In the final years I want the assurance that my existence is resting on a solid bed of knowledge. Of course, I realize that my library will bear little resemblance to the great libraries of Alexandria or the Vatican. But its purpose will be the same. The one advantage it will have over those great enterprises is that it will have those idiosyncratic touches that reflect my unique character, my particular reception of the vast offerings of history and the world. For example, although I have a sufficient representation of scientific achievements, I have an unparalleled representation of the lives of the Bushmen of the Kalahari Desert in South West Africa. My wife has often wondered about that, as have I occasionally, but I cite it merely to illustrate. As the great change comes ever nearer, I find that I am thinking more about the adjustments I will make from my current arrangement, and there is some anxiety here. Perhaps if I list some of my concerns, it will clarify what I am planning to do, what I want to accomplish.

1.     For example, my current arrangement is quite scattered. There are books in every room, stacked and inserted in every which way, according to how and when I acquired them and according to space considerations. Increasingly, books in one room are connected with books in other rooms, and increasingly I must rummage to find what I want. To fit new books in where I think they belong would require impossible upheavals. Sometimes a book will "disappear" for months, only to reappear in another quest. Sometimes, thinking a book truly lost, lent (but to whom?), or stolen, I have bought another, and so end up with two copies. Periodically, in a burst of efficiency and order, I sift through my books, plucking out those I think I might store in boxes (labeled, of course) in a closet or basement. Although this creates room for new acquisitions, I worry about losing or losing sight of the ones removed. Accessibility is an important matter with me. I also worry about my reasons for removing them. Although not quite an amputation, it does seem a loss of something. But what? Unfortunately, I cannot deal with everything. Having an entire room designated as a library would, it seems to me, eliminate such problems, or at least alleviate them.

2.     *Taxonomies, etc.* Just as all things are separated into cate-

gories, so, too, it seems to me, ought books. The problem is how. When I was very young I leaned toward the symmetry of color and size in my bookkeeping (I rejected thickness), but then I grew up. So, too, the world; we rest upon layers of rejected taxonomies, a psychic palimpsest that sometimes invades our sleep. It would be simpler, of course, if books had genitalia. Thus a history creature could not be shelved with a physics creature. Unfortunately, it is not so simple. Sometimes physics is history, or something else. In some cases, physics might not even be physics. Guidance is difficult to come by here; taxonomies sooner or later become quaint. And mistakes—if there can be such—can be fatal. The Mesopotamian Empire, for example, could disappear. Some time ago I thought simple alphabetization by author might solve all problems. But that left the problems of editors, and of multiple authors (where the second or third is more noted than the first), and of anthologies to deal with. Also, quite often I seek a particular book but cannot remember the author. The other alternative, obviously, is shelving by subject, vague and dangerous as that is, and that is my present arrangement. However, as I have hinted above, *subject* can be a confusing realm. A disquisition on the differences between Tolstoy and Dostoevsky as writers might be literature (subheading Russian), or literary theory, or history, or philosophy, or something other. Where would it go? A section (or a wall?) for anomalies? There is an argument to be made, I recognize, for all categories to be considered anomalies. Here, perception is everything. But perception itself is anomalous. The whole idea of cross references, too, is an endless swamp. At any rate, to move on, my allocations are easily disrupted, and when, say, my art history space, such as it is, is packed, I have no choice but to seek a few inches or feet in another shelf, room, or hallway, or possibly to establish a sub-category, just as the Alder Flycatcher (*Empidonax alnorum*), although indistinguishable from the Willow Flycatcher (*Empidonax traillii*) and once called by the same name (Thaill's Flycatcher), might in fact be considered a subspecies, if not another species entirely. Just incidentally, it might be noted that having books all over the apartment also creates certain domestic and living problems. Aside from the problem of dusting and cleaning, there is the problem of the walls behind the books. At a certain point it becomes impossible even to think of cleaning and painting them. Removal (and then replacement) of the books would most certainly be traumatic. It is either move abode entirely or nothing. Only when books are decorative can they be removed for painting (which raises another subject entirely). Obviously a home with a library eliminates a certain domestic stress, although the problem remains *within* the library itself. Unless, perhaps, the shelves are built into the wall itself. I suppose there is still the question of whether or not *all* books (and all allocations, for that matter) are decorative. That question does not seem relevant, however, to my present purpose, unless it is all *too* relevant, in which case certainly not discussible here.

3.   *Space and allocation.* This is always difficult. At one point in my life, for example, I would have had no space for my Kalahari books, or at the most a very small space within a larger category (Ethnicities? Geography? Anthropology? Exotica? Utopias? Autobiography?) How much can I predict my future interests? The world changes every day, every moment. In my conception of a new library, there is a certain tranquility. This presumes (or allows for) some accommodation to the flux of life, but not too much. Too much would defeat my purposes. The room, of course, is large. There are shelves on all the walls, from floor to ceiling, except for where I shall have a painting or two, a horse perhaps, on a foggy morning. There are not, however, rows of shelves bisecting my space, as in, say, public or university libraries, although that would be practical, if not restful. No, my idea of a library requires comfortable furniture, a desk, maybe a wood filing cabinet (for what?). A rug or two, of course, and good lamps. A lectern for consulting large volumes and a tasteful small ladder. I would not necessarily need a window. It is a room into which I will come, select a well-bound book easily, and sink into something, be it Egyptology or some new category I have devised to encompass my collection and my needs. But how full are the

shelves? My true library requires that almost all space be utilized. After all, what is a library if not complete or nearly so? A library should be a reflection of a foundation and must be solidly and amply shelved, with large areas of completeness, to give comfort. Such have they been throughout history, as many great paintings attest, and many a professional enclosure, like the law office. A little space may be left for addenda. Exactly where and how much is a bit of a problem. Some small categories, for example, might mushroom as a result of some ragged pilgarlic in Gdansk or Central Asia, and my own brain is still something of a mystery to me. I do have a nagging anxiety about what I will do if the books ever exceed the spaces I have allocated or the dimensions of the library itself. And once, for example, the library itself is designated as a category, what, then, will be a kitchen or a bedroom? May books enter or not? Sacrilege or disorder of some sort is at hand. Space must be carefully preserved.

4.     *Current books.* I have been contemplating a special section of books I use frequently, along with new acquisitions and interests. This would run somewhat along the lines of my current disorganized and scattered collection. But it would be more limited in space, and therefore, although I would rummage, I would not run much risk of getting lost or wasting time. The bottom shelf of this section might possibly be for my duplicate copies, although

with my new system there would be fewer of these. Of course, as certain of the books in this section became, so to speak, used up, I would file them in my regular library. But, having said that, I am concerned that, in a sense, I will have *two* libraries, my main library and within that a miniature of my former library, one my living library, so to speak again, and the other a repository (of dead books?). This is disquieting.

What I should now be doing is gathering my books from their various slots and boxing them appropriately. I am not doing that. I have a secret conviction that as soon as I set up my new library I shall die. I shall sit in my comfortable chair, my lamp focused, surrounded by my perfect arrangement, and die. (What will there be to live for?) This, clearly, is ridiculous. Of course I cannot tell my wife about this. Just yesterday I put a small bookcase in the bathroom, and she looked at me queerly. The new house is suddenly looming as a monstrosity. My wife is very excited and talking about wallpaper, paint, fabric, furniture. I am thinking tomb. Have I become suddenly, oddly, mad? If she were to enter where I am now, she would find me sitting like a nincompoop, staring at a young woman of the Kalahari. She is naked from the waist up. There is an extraordinary curve in her back, which the caption describes as a typical case of *steatopygia*. I whip out my dictionary (I have one in every room). Soon I am weighing *lordosic* and *callipygian* against *steatopygian* and wondering what it might mean, whatever it is (and it is *enormous*). Am I on the verge of some new category? A half dozen books are at my feet. I have been sitting on a low stool, ruminating for nearly an hour, in a metaphysical trance. Where, I wonder, is my map of Africa? Why have I never put a bookshelf in the front hall closet? Sooner or later, my wife will come in, and I shall be exposed, utterly exposed. What will I tell her? What are the words?

# SUBWAY I

1.  On the subway one day a crowd of people near the center door. Police. They are removing the body of a young woman. Pretty in a conventional way, but a large part of one side of her face eaten away. And very stiff. They cannot bend her out of her sitting position. She seems very light and dry, almost baked. Spanish, I think. Her clothing is cheap but with flair. Several smaller figures near her, possibly children. And people who have vomited or fainted. One is still vomiting. This is really getting him in the gut. It is something of a stir, yet controlled, organized. The police are carrying on. The train is not delayed long. Several thoughts: the stiffness—it was striking. And she must have been on the train several days. Was it still safe to let the children use the subway? Would it be in the newspaper? Probably not.

2.  So when she woke, it was all strange to her. They told her it had been fourteen days. Fourteen days of *what*? she said. It was obvious she was angry. They all looked at one another. Look, your kids are dead, one of them said. She didn't scream, and they had expected her to. What a piece, they were all thinking. Would

you like to see my cunt? she asked. She didn't beat around the bush. Slut, one of them said. And she laughed. When she laughed she did not look like such a piece, because her teeth were rotten. But it didn't bother her. She felt the same, laughing or not. Maria Theresa Garcia, she said, and showed them her cunt. *Mira, mira,* they said, though they were not Spanish. I am twenty-eight, she continued. Which of you has a hard-on? No one answered, so she covered it up. And then they thought about it. Crooked, off-pink, wrinkled, hairy, and sort of bunched up and pouting just before her buttocks. It was a cunt, all right. And what an ass. It was all very vivid and they made sly smiles at one another. You are all cock-suckers, she said, and one of them slapped her so hard on the bad side of her face that a rotten tooth fell out. Dirty Spic piece of ass, he said. They all laughed again. Where are my children? she asked. Show us your cunt again, they said, and laughed. Will you eat it? she asked, and laughed back. Your children are dead, they said. So am I, she answered. They broke off her brittle limbs and packed them neatly in a box with her torso. They plucked out her cunt and put it in a glass of water and kept it on a desk. Once a Spic always a Spic.

3.   On the subway, forty-two people saw her. Three of them vomited, one fainted. Thirty were women, ten were men, two were children. Three policemen had handled the matter. The only

mess was from the three who vomited, and that was cleaned that night. By morning it was a fresh start.—And there she is again, Maria Theresa Garcia. See? See? *Mira, mira. Mira* Maria Theresa Garcia. Does she have her cunt? You'll never know.

# SUBWAY II

1.   Now this one is Pedro. And he says to her, "You are a stupid fuck." "I will cut off your balls," she says, and he slaps her. So she begins carrying a razor around with her.

2.   But meanwhile he is fucking her regularly, and she likes it. She appears to forget, but she does not. Pedro thinks she has forgot, and that is one of the reasons he thinks she is a stupid fuck. Which is, incidentally, the way he likes her. But he is wrong and he is stupid. Some nights, just to add spice, she fucks with the razor under the pillow. And when she climaxes she makes a long sibilant sound which is like a razor cutting. "What is this new jazz!" he asks her one night. She does not tell him.

3.   Pedro is very proud of his cock, especially when it is erect. It is like a true friend, and he often strokes and pats it. Mostly it is just a friendly gesture, but also partly to keep it in shape. He doesn't wear underwear, and his tight pants keep him excited all day. Girls look at the lump on his leg when he sits on the subway. He sees forty or fifty a day he could fuck on the spot.

## The Man in the Stretcher

By nightfall he is well primed to go. And so is she.

4     After four times Pedro is sleeping. Then he feels her hand on him and smiles as he grows big. *Señor,* which is what he calls his cock, never fails him. Then he hears the sibilant sound and for a split second he is disturbed: the sequence is wrong. Then he sits up with a cry of pain, his hand, clutching his crotch. She is standing there with his bloody balls in her hand. She smiles, drops the razor, and leaves. Pedro, in a state of shock, gets into his pants and takes a taxi to the hospital, where they sew him up. His greatest anger at that moment is that she took his balls with her. He thinks if he had them they might be sewn on again.

5.     Pedro now wears looser pants on the subway. He has told no one about his accident. He also carries the razor. In another car *she* carries the balls in her purse. If anyone calls her a stupid fuck she will take them out and dangle them.

6.     She misses Pedro's cock. Pedro misses it, too. He has never cleaned the razor. Where will it all end?

# SUBWAY III

1.     Dancing Tiger. Alfredo the Dancing Tiger. He is called that because he loves to dance. Even when he fights he dances. And he is a good fighter,

2.     Manuel, on the other hand, can't dance at all. But he is a mean fighter. And has no girlfriends. He would like to kill Alfredo, but everyone likes him, especially the girls. Also, he cannot find any pretext to kill Alfredo,

3.     One day they meet. "Hey, man," says Manuel. "Hey, man, watcha doin'?" says Alfredo. "Hey, man, you Dancing Tiger, huh?" says Manuel. They are both prancing on the balls of their feet. "Yeah, man," says Alfredo, " I dance 'em, then I fuck 'em. Never fails, man." "Hey, cool, man, real cool," says Manuel, who is boiling. Alfredo knows he is boiling and he is enjoying it. "Hey, man," he says, "got this cool, cool chick the other night, wouldn't put out shit, man, for nobody. Danced her ass off, *man*, she was a cool hot fuck, let me tell ya, man." "Yeah. Dancing Tiger strikes again, hey, man?" says Manuel. "Yeah, you get it, man," says

Alfredo. "Real cool." And they slap hands and part.

4.   Well, Manuel didn't get anything out of that exchange, and he goes home and masturbates.

5.   The next day, on the subway, he sees a blind man waiting for a train. The train stops, and the blind man is half way between two doors. Manuel takes his arm and says, "Mister, the door is over here." At which the blind man swings his cane in a rage and shrieks, "Don't help me!" Manuel is paralyzed for a moment at the outburst, and then he kicks the blind man in the balls. "Fucken jerk!" he yells, "I'm trying to *help* you!" The blind man is lying on the platform groping for his cane, and Manuel is arrested.

6.   When Dancing Tiger hears about it he shakes his head and mutters, "Man, that Manuel, he is *crazy*."

7.   In jail, Manuel masturbates again.

# IMPOSSIBLE LITANIES, NECESSARY ACT[ION]S

1.      If you drop something, why pick it up? That is my tendency, of course. Fat Spider is watching, and although I don't need it or need it right away, I don't want to be gobbled up. So I pick it up immediately. And just who is Fat Spider, you might ask? And I say, you may ask, but I won't tell you. I'm not sure I *can* tell you.

2.      If you are late, why go at all? Nothing can change the fact. Of course, you will say is it not better late than not at all? Also, if you do not go, what then will you do? Not necessarily anything. You can simply stand where you are in a state of lateness, whatever that might be. And of course you are not late for your state of lateness. So it is a standoff between you and Fat Spider. As long as you don't move, she won't eat you. And when the occasion for which you are late ends, then you and Fat Spider both fade away, retire. It has been trying, but life goes on. However, if you should go somewhere else during the period for which you are late, wherever you arrive, you are not late, but Fat Spider is chasing you, and you might well panic. Sometimes you can throw a line to where you were supposed to be and climb there hand over

hand. Fat Spider is watching you but won't follow too closely. You wipe a lot of sweat from your brow when you arrive and wonder whether it was worth it. You might well make it a point not to be late again, even though the not-late-other-place or the never-late-other-place lingers pleasantly in your mind. But not for long.

3.   Fat Spider's specialty, of course, is spinning webs. When you lose your train of thought, Fat Spider's web helps you to pick it up. It is usually stuck somewhere nearby. But if you don't try to pick it up, if you just go wandering, you might get all wrapped up, enmeshed, until you wouldn't recognize yourself. Fat Spider is reserving you for a later meal.

4.   Probably the best thing is to study Fat Spider a lot, whether she's called Ruthie or Apple-Dumpling or anything else. Then you learn to scurry along the web as she does, nimble and fleet-footed. Such familiarity need not breed contempt, only a comforting indifference to Fat Spider, misplaced though it might be.

5.   One problem, though, is she can spin a web and you can't. Also, she never falls and you do. If she *seems* to fall, you will always notice a silvery strand behind her that is always enough

for her to climb back on. But if you fall, where do you fall and how hard do you hit? And when Ruthie is facing you there (as she would be), what do you do? What *can* you do?

6.  Another problem is that even though Ruthie is watching you all the time and you and she seem to exist in some fundamental relationship, you and she are not really constituted the same way. It is very unlikely that you have ever thought of yourself as a smaller spider, although the possibility certainly exists. The closest you might come to that is when, in imitating Ruthie, you scurry along her web. But when you fall and she does not, you realize there is a fundamental difference. The only thing you know at that point is that she is very likely going to eat you and that somehow it is related to your falling. She will incorporate you and become even fatter and stronger. And you will disappear. Ruthie counts, and you do not.

7.  Does this mean that Ruthie subsists mainly or entirely on the bodies of those who fall? If nobody fell, would Ruthie exist? Would Ruthie need to exist? Probably, in both cases, and although she might appear to have lost interest in you, she hasn't. She knows something very important that you do not, namely that she *precedes* you.

8.    It happens that my wife has a friend who was once a Jew in Germany. She doesn't eat anything, except sometimes when she laughs. It is a laugh she learned in a very hard way in a very hard time, and although she practices it on a lot of people, it does not impress Fat Spider.

9.    Sometimes, if you feel a little crazy or desperate, you might think you, too, can spin a web. But if you tried to do it, it would look suspiciously like moving your bowels, or vomiting, or bleeding. It isn't something you could scurry easily on, although it might be worth a try, and some few have done so, with notable failure.

10. Although Fat Spider doesn't *need* to eat you, she always can.

11. Some people have tried to put Fat Spider to sleep with song, but Ruthie never sleeps. The least tug on her web and she is one hundred percent alert. We, on the other hand, are often put to sleep by song, and sometimes we lose our footing.

12. Fat Spider's web goes from horizon to horizon, and there is nothing underneath it, at least nothing we recognize or understand.

13.     When my wife's friend laughs, she shows all her teeth. She has a very special way of laughing *at* things. I think she is pretending to be Fat Spider. But she isn't, of course. She has fallen once, lived to tell the tale, and does not want to fall again.

14.     It is only lately that I have thought of not picking up something I have dropped. It is only lately that I have noticed Ruthie watching me.

15. Yesterday I did not answer the telephone and felt sick.

16. The day before yesterday I ate out of a dish I had not washed.

17. I don't know what to call the day before the day before yesterday. I cannot say Tuesday. Tuesday is meaningless to me. A great deal is meaningless to me.

18.     I'm pretty sure I'm falling and that Ruthie is dangling on a slim thread behind me. How much thread can she spin?

19.     I'm also trying to pronounce a word, but I don't know what it is.

20. And my mind keeps telling me that Ruthie is Apple-

Dumpling, Ruthie is Apple-Dumpling, Ruthie is only Apple-Dumpling….

21. Nevertheless, I cannot rid myself of the feeling that I am falling, falling as in a dream that will not end. Fat Spider is close behind me, fetid and intense. She has eyes only for me, and it is making life difficult, perhaps…impossible. Yes, at any moment, my life will be impossible.

# NEWS STORY

I was struck, at first, by the music. I thought it might be the weather because the music was spring-like. But then it became heavy Spanish chords. A terrorist bomb had exploded in a square and killed three. What square? What country? Apparently that was not important. What was important were the three people—a mother, her three year old child, and a man without an identity. The child was essentially thoughtless and without personality. He had lost three limbs. The mother, a pretty divorcee in her early thirties, had been on the lookout for a new romance in her life. We'll come back to the stranger later. Thirteen organizations proudly claimed responsibility for the act. I decided the music was terrorist death music. It was quickly followed by American Beauty Queen music. A pageant was in progress. Fifty beautiful teens representing all of our states were wearing bathing suits and smiling. Suddenly the terrorist death music broke in and someone presented the baby with three bleeding stumps to Miss Teen Ohio. She screamed. Blood came out of her mouth. Before anyone realized what was happening, her screaming face appeared on several million screens. Sponsors were outraged. Miss Teen Ohio was dragged backstage, and her bloody bathing suit was ripped from her body. It was clear she had no chance of winning the contest. She was left a quivering teen mass on the floor, lipstick smeared, mascara running, lewdly observed by the stage crew. No one knew what happened to the baby. In fact, most people doubted there had even been a baby. Later in the day, during the newscast, they were showing clips of the terrorist bombing, accompanied by the same heavy Spanish chords. Suddenly they segued into American Beauty Queen music, and Miss Teen America (not Miss Teen Ohio, who had slithered off in a rag) appeared in the square like a vision. She was wearing a bathing suit and she was smiling. But the smile went on too long. The camera would not leave her. She looked confused, as if she were dressed inappropriately or had not plucked her pubic hair enough. Then there was cereal music, toothpaste music, and Caribbean holiday music. Miss Teen America stood next to a little black child happily crunching cereal, then a faded movie star extolling the family value of paste for her false teeth, and finally a shipload of happy aged revelers, also in bathing suits and apparently staring at the moon as they danced madly. Obviously, Miss Teen America thought, it was all part of the promotion she had contracted for. She had better keep smiling, she thought. Then, for a brief moment, she was back in the American Beauty Queen Pageant and felt better. This was what her mother had raised her for. This was what it was all about. Her smile was sparkling. One of the judges squeezed her buttock and asked if she would fuck him. She was confused, and turned, her wet mouth open. The judge was a she, and in her hard dry-turf look there was a serious question. Then the heavy Spanish chords returned and she was in the square again, sweating. The baby had evidently found its way back and was lying a few feet from her, its glazed eyes staring at her. She wondered how, with three limbs missing, its face was so unmarked. She decided to strike a pose. She bent one knee, inhaled and held her shoulders back, and thrust out her pelvis. It was a classic pose, giving maximum nipple effect and lots of reproductive promise to her hips. She was wetting her lips when the bomb exploded. The baby flew into her arms, and she fell to the ancient paving stones, covered with blood. The third victim, the man without identification, was lying next to her. He was very handsome, in the Mediterranean way, with dark eyes, a moustache, and dark coloring. He turned his head to her, languidly, and said, "You are very beautiful. Will you marry me? We will have many beautiful children." She was very affected by the proposal, awkward as it was, but she had her career to think of. Latin romance could come later. She was about to tell him so, when his eyes went dead. Then there was weight-loss music for women who had tried everything. It was a clever promotional for very agile fat women led by a monkey. Although she could not get up, she smiled. Something was wrong with her teeth. She pushed the baby aside and tried to make her body seductive, bloody as it was. It did not respond. It didn't matter, she thought. A night's beauty rest and she would be ready to go. And she would go far. She was Miss Teen Arizona and she had won. The heavy Spanish terrorist music sounded again. She smiled faintly and closed her eyes. She was very tired, numb, in fact. They took pictures of her. She was on every screen. It was the way she had always dreamed it. Poor Miss Teen Ohio. How green she must be.

# A FEW WORDS, A LITTLE SHELTER

*"Names arise only when there is something living to denote."*
 —Cees Nooteboom, *The Following Story*

If there can be the voice of nothing, why can there not be the name of nothing? May not a name of nothing add something, bring it into being? Most assuredly this is so. How else could we praise illuminati like Freud, like Darwin, Marx, and a host of others? Where is the face of the unconscious? Or the dictatorship of the proletariat? Of course such creations may also weaken and die, become merely history, awaiting another great, or mad-, man's touch. Or maybe not. Surely in our quotidian lives we create more from nothing than we rely on the something there. We do not, simply, have the time or the energy or the skill to fabricate the names. Perhaps we thereby retain these things better, a name being always brutal. But sometimes we yearn for shorthand, for reduction, as a currency for living, for society.

For example, if a shovel handle is placed across the throat of a lying man and one then stomps upon it until the neck is broken and life extinguished, should there not be a name for it? It is enough merely to describe the frailty and desperation of the man, the indifference and health of the stomper, the dimensions of the shovel? Obviously not, just as "murder" or "brutality" will not do. Perhaps something of the quality of the earth, the details of the lives of men, the time of year and day, the weather, and so on would help. But not enough. Eventually one must realize that each naming negates, or at the very least negotiates, the history of the world, enlarges the void, and if one cannot listen to the silent syllables, the sounds of infinite disarray, one knows nothing, one barely skims a surface. One dies as one pretends to live.

For example, someone I know is dying—in the other sense, I mean. We are all dying, of course, but that cliché, like the word "dying" itself, tells us little. It is only the particulars of a dying that can reveal the many syllables of the unheard word, the word that can be used only once, for this dying alone. I will not name him, for to call him Harry, or Egbert, or Sylvester, is immediately to trivialize him. But be sure he has a name, as he has a wife and children. He has also done some fine, maybe even great, things.

"I'm glad," he says, after another of our long silences, "that you don't try to say too much."

We are indeed, good friends. "No," I say, "there isn't too much to say. Despite the psychologists."

He laughs. "Damn the psychologists! Damn them all!"

Silently, I do. Psychologists are the metaphysicians of accommodation, epistemologists of the banal. The less I say about my friend, the more I know. The more we share.

"What is quite clear," he says, "is that we can't live forever. That's ... unfortunate."

"Perhaps," I say, "we can die forever."

He likes that, and laughs. Sputters, I should say. I know we are both thinking that it would be good if we could find some expression to describe the loss or the friendship or the achievement. He soon falls asleep. His breathing is labored. No doubt his thoughts, his dreams, are tangled. More non-words. How thin he has become, I think. And he has never lost his teeth.

His wife comes in. She raises her eyebrows in question. I smile. Waiting for a friend to die is to feel deeply a fool in the universe.

"The children," I say. "How are they?"

"Immortal," she says. "And frightened. He is not their father."

"No," I answer. "They are on a threshold of a knowledge."

"Too young?" I ask.

"One can never be too young. For anything."

I think about what she is saying.

"You mean," I say, "that one could hardly live, otherwise. The unsayable words are always there, waiting."

"Yes. The unsayable words."

I fidget. Then I almost laugh, thinking, "I've got the fidgets." It is like a song. Should I get up and dance the tune? She would recognize me, I think. She smiles at me, thinking, I am sure, that I am a fool, but a fool she can tolerate. We are all fools. "Would you like some tea?" she asks. I nod. Even fools like us sometimes acquiesce to a few words, a little shelter.

## PROLEGOMENA

Let us grant that anything I say may be used against me.

Let us grant that whatever I say it is all untrue but may for various expediencies be accepted as true, that we are entered here, as in an unholy matrimony, into an agreement to play the game, abiding by its rules, and pretending to enjoy its satisfactions, breath by dying breath.

Let us grant that this pretense is no different from any other pretense, except that it is understood that some games are considered better than others but opinions vary as to which.

Let us grant that although I claim to be the author of these words and am reading them, I do not exist.

Let us grant that although I do not exist, neither do I wish to be harmed. Even so, if I bleed, I will continue to deny that I exist, even as I continue to admit that I wrote these words and seek medical care for myself.

Let us grant, however, that I do not claim to write (or speak) these words in blood.

Let us grant that you do not exist either. Although you are listening and responding to what I read, you have no understanding of it because you do not know what it is. Further, you are each responding differently to what you don't understand, but because of the seating arrangement, the ticket price, the program, and other such formalities it might seem that you share something or that we share something or that there is something to share.

Let us grant that even if you blow each other's brains out you still do not exist, even if with your last breath you claim to understand what I am not the author of and ask for a decent and civilized burial.

Let us grant that if a cat were to walk across the stage, it might or might not exist. However, the word "cat" walking across the stage might more likely exist, just as the name Mr. Jones might more likely exist than the assemblage it is temporarily attached to.

Let us grant that my wife, who is sitting amongst you, does not exist even though she is the mother of three non-existent children, who claim me as a non-existent father.

Let us grant that if I strangled the cat and in expiring the cat tore my face to shreds, something might exist, the same way anything else might exist, but no one could say what it is because no one is here and even if someone were here he would not be sure of what he was seeing, namely only a dying cat disfiguring a non-existent author.

Let us grant that no one would probably be impervious to

my screams, my blood and the dead cat dumped in his lap. This would be true even if his name were Mr. Jones, Mr. Harold Jones, Jonesy, or Diddle-Dump.

Let us grant that insofar as we can imagine the cat's brain the cat probably felt that he existed and also felt that he was ceasing to exist.

Let us grant that had the cat not thought so he would probably not have scratched my face.

Let us grant that if the cat remains dead in the auditorium for three days, even though he might not exist he will smell.

Let us grant that if a woman were lying on a psychoanalyst's couch and she were being fucked by a baboon she would have several grounds for doubting that it was happening.

Let us grant that even so she might have troubling thoughts. But let us grant also that if she told her non-existent husband they could have a good laugh over it.

Let us grant that although the reading of these words I did not write occurs within a certain space and time, your existence within it is purely arbitrary.

Let us grant that this time may in fact be no time or designated as the triple stretching of a cockroach's wing or anything else.

Let us grant that "grant" means nothing and nothing is binding between us.

Let us grant that if I said "let us grant" with enough feeling I could say anything and accompany it with appropriate music.

Let us grant that I could introduce three pigs into the narration if I wished.

Let us grant, however, that I could assume no responsibility for them.

Let us grant that the cat, the baboon, and the pigs are hard to grasp, that the game which includes them must have unusual rules, and that not too many people want to, or can, play by them, especially because it's easy to make mistakes or comparisons, and a comparison is often as bad as a mistake. In other words, a pig in a poke could be death staring you in the face.

Let us grant that the presentation could go on forever but that in limiting it I am accomplishing something.

Let us grant that although neither I nor you are really here and that this time does not exist it is possible that you might get hungry, or tired, and go home and that my awareness of this, for which I take no credit, helps to shape what it is we're not really experiencing.

Let us grant that in fact we could all of us fuck baboons with impunity.

Let us grant, however, that if we had baboons in Congress, there would be penalties (or rewards), at least until they were voted out.

Let us grant that if you said "I hurt" I might be skeptical, I might withhold medication, I might even "hurt" you more to see how much you don't exist and how much your "pain" might be something else, which has no name, for there is no place for it to be.

Let us grant that "I" and "you" may or may not be "out there" floating somewhere, that we may even be the same, and that same a part of something hitherto designated as "cosmic pork chop," although that is certainly wrong or at least inadequate but all we have for the "moment" and further that if I suggest that it is a cosmic pork chop perturbation instead of pain that you feel you might not only have difficulty in understanding me but want even to kill or harm me, even though I do not exist, because I am making life difficult for you.

Let us grant that what you see on my face are what are called tears and that I see the same on yours, but do not make the mistake of thinking they are what you think they are or that you understand them or that they mean anything at all. They are something happening after and not because of other things are happening, and still other things will happen, but they may all be happening at once or in reverse, or in some other way, or not at all. We don't exist, we don't know. We only think we are in this theater in the midst of this thing with these salty drops curling into our mouths, with these cannonadings within the skin that is not we, not wee-wee, not not, not not not, and certainly not. So therefore and finally….

Epilog: Some Alternatives and Other Options
1.	Let us, Grant. The story of a stern step-father, an obsessed older brother, or
2.	Lettuce Grant. The courageous story of the making of a new salad hybrid, or Congress's strange appropriation.
3.	"Lettuce" Grant. Never the nickname of our 18th president and its influence on history.
4.	Let Us Grant, I. The inside story of the salvation army. An as-told-to saga.
5.	Lett-U.S. Grant. The strange history of our Balto-Slavic venture in World War II.
6.	Let Us Grant, II. The Rockefellers and the Guggenheims: a century of endowment or the Lord's Prayer, revised.
7.	Lettuce, Grant. A forgiving wife bestows salad upon her erring husband.
8.	*[Tu] le tues*, Grant. How a man named Grant led his younger brother by the nose into three despicable practices.
9.	*Tue[s]-le*, Grant. The story of a Parisian rub-out.
10.	Where did the baboon come from and where did it go?
11.	To whom did the cat/non-cat belong? Was the name "cat"

three-dimensional? The dying cat as tragedy, or what has been accomplished so far.

12. The sexes of the three pigs and why.

15.* Sara's cystic breasts twenty-five years ago in Cairo (tel. communication).

16. Epistemology vs. Episeotomy: fatal dichotomies.

17. Glory to the King [K]ing, K[ing], or K[in]g.

18. When all is sad and done: death as the not-is.

19. This is a perfectly good sentence. And this is

The End of Ends [

* #13 and #14 have been abolished.

# THRIFT

Parsimony is in my blood. I toast the end pieces of a loaf. I get triple my money back from clothing wear. I am constantly orchestrating my movements to save time. "So, how come you had four children?" my eleven-year-old daughter quite rightly asks. Can I properly answer her?—tell her, for example, that one knows that not all children live, and if one wants a family one hedges against fate? It suddenly strikes me as horrendous that I am implying the death of one out of four would be less grievous than the death of an *only* child. What child could ever understand, or forgive, that—knowing that he or she might be so chosen? Looking at her, I want to cry. How grateful I am that she cannot read my stupid thought. "Well?" she prods. I give another reason. "In some things it doesn't do to be thrifty." "What things?" she asks. I can answer her, but I don't think she can properly understand or apply what I would say. "Your mother and I were only children," I say. "We wanted a different kind of family." She ponders and says nothing. It sits right with her. So I venture more. "We live in a crazy world also, I say. "We thought it would be nice to add some sane people to it." Again I am struck by my presumption and stupidity. She is right after me. "But you're always calling *us* crazy." I laugh. "It's a different thing," I say. "Sure, sure," she retorts, "everything's a different thing." There is no getting into that statement. I look at her and think not so much that we are having a discussion, that she is intelligent, as that in her still small body, in her head, cells are functioning, organs, muscles. She digests food. She *works*. "Is Mommy going to die?" she asks. "We all are," I answer. "*You know what I mean.*" She asks in a schoolroom way, but it is a very serious question, one she has been trying to find an off-hand occasion for. "We're not sure yet," I say. "There are more tests. But it looks good right now." She is watching me like a very intense bird. I want to smile, I want to hug her, I want to cry. I can do none of them. She is wondering whether I am being thrifty, whether I can be trusted. I wait. Finally she says, "I don't think I would have four children. In fact, I don't think I'll have *any* children." "It's too early to say definitely," I say. "People change their minds." "Well, *I* won't." She gets up and puts a record on the machine, a silly teenage group. She moves gracefully, with directness and purpose. I pretend to read the newspaper, but watch her, my heart full. She pretends to ignore me and listens to the music, but watches to see whether I am looking at her with any special look. We are going through another day.

# LOSING GROUND

A famous recluse and cynic, recently deceased, once wrote, "It's not worth the bother of killing yourself, since you always kill yourself *too late*." Indeed, that is so, and therefore cheering. The only blow to be struck against the exigencies of fate must precede pain and despair, be executed in the midst of health and happiness. And this, as we all know, is difficult, for it goes against some deeply human yearning in us to endure, especially in the midst of our contentments. I have discussed this with my wife, and although she accedes to the logic of my cynic, she is wary of and uncomfortable with the discourse itself. For example, I think it bothers her that I am struck by it, even delighted. For what, she thinks, is so delightful about such a strategy? Why bother, then, to be born at all? Indeed. I quickly urge upon her another aphorism, namely, "To live is to lose ground," and then laugh, no doubt hideously. This does not raise her spirits, in part because her birthday is approaching. I realize, far too late, that I have once again transgressed into forbidden territory. For we do have our differences. I, for example, am awash with mortality. She, on the other hand, lives in an immortality of silence, which can often be charming, except in the dead of night. Mostly, as you can well understand, I ponder the issue privately, for it is really quite extensive philosophically. Just about any venture, any action, is quite open to morbid speculations, if such they be, and perfect stasis can seem Edenic. Now, of course, one can approach the ridiculous in weighing the risks of peeling a peach or planning a picnic. One should program oneself, to a reasonable degree, to be carefree in life, to cross streets and meadow with some unalloyed sense of joy, even exuberance. And there, I must admit, I am wanting, warning my wife of curbs and the cavities of small mammals, so to speak, raising orthopedic and other specters in the midst of life's succulence. And yet, how can I not? We endure mainly by virtue of our blindness, endlessly elaborated, as so many millions have discovered to their anguish. So often, lately, at one social event or another, I find myself staring at one human performer or another, blabbering away about the wonders of himself or herself, and seeing slow growths beneath the skin or basilisks beyond the door, awaiting them, or me. Yet I know that *he* loves his children dearly and *she* is an advocate of many good causes, like the feeding of starving children in distant lands. Why do I want, at such moments, to laugh or to cry? Have *I* gone beyond some pale? I protest not. What I want, after all, is merely some moderation, some hint of democratic fear, an Hawthornian recognition of that frail boat in which we all reside, so that I might extend my hand, my embrace, in fellowship, perhaps whispering, "What a monster you are." Indeed, I am quite eager to love most people. But I know I should be rejected as some slimy beastie from the deep. How *dare* I presume fellowship on such a basis. And my wife, seeing me stare, will think me simply awful, an eruption of social solecism to be quickly stoppered with food and drink or chatty discourse, like the true ends of society. I am. of course, agreeable. Life must go on, bloodshed or no. I have even, at such moments, come close to dancing, which would throw everyone into a funk, for it would be a strange dancing, indeed. Sometimes, on these grim occasions, my wife is liable to hold my hand tightly, not so much as a restraint but as a communication, as if to say, "For god's sake. I know everything, but must we live with it every second? Can we not pretend and get through some of it without your monumental fussing?" It is then that I am likely to realize what a wonderful woman she is and vow never to let her out of my sight, even for a moment, for all moments are awful. But, of course, I will. I do. Every absence is a cause for tears, but we must carefully hide them. There are tears in everything. And there is nothing we can do about it, unless we heed our recluse, now no longer suffering.

## NULLITY

I have just made an amazing discovery. I am in the habit of recording some of my choice thoughts with the typewriter. And for years it has been of passing interest that each word, each letter, in fact, is lighter than the previous one. This is because the ribbon gradually wears out. And if I type long enough on one ribbon, the result would be nullity. This is true even were I to increase the striking pressure on the keyboard. Nullity, though delayed, is inevitable. Now this attrition I gradually realized to be a useful metaphor for much, maybe most, of the workings of our society. All mechanical means move towards a condition of nullity—unless (and here is a major point), unless we replace or repair them. It is what makes our civilization go around. To avoid nullity, we replace and repair. The charm of the process is the gradual but inevitable drift downward. To prevent it we must exert ourselves and we must spend. That is, we must exploit our finite life force, a bio-depletion, and we must create a system for the exercise of that exploitation, call it economics, society, or what you will. Thus, each time I have purchased a new ribbon to crank up, so to speak, the wear and tear of life and civilization, I have felt a certain pleasure in participating in a process rooted, surely, to the very bowels of our history. To be sure, there were times when I felt a certain unease, a cranky desire, for example, *not* to change the ribbon, to continue typing my thoughts in ever fainter impressions. Who could say when, exactly, I had achieved absolute nullity, crossed some fateful border? And even though invisible to the ordinary eye, might not my script still continue to exist, even far into some ultimate pit? That is, who can discriminate the degrees of invisibility? And are not many of life's scripts written within such?

    Now this, to be sure, is very heady stuff. Perhaps even dangerous. And I am not, as a rule, prone to upsetting applecarts. I *create* applecarts; I am useful and productive. So for the most part, I regularly purchased my new ribbon, content to bear my load in life (or death). However, a recent change in that life has pushed me to the edge of radical new assessments. For Christmas my wife and children, of whom I'm fond, bought me a new typewriter. At first I was delighted. But then, as I realized what I had received, I became disturbed, distressed even. The crux is this: my new typewriter has no ribbon attrition. Each letter can be struck only once per place. The ribbon is not reusable. When used once, it must be discarded and a new one bought. *Every letter, every word, is exactly the same* since they partake equally of the ribbon. It was a complete destruction of my working metaphysics (and everyone, I think, should have a working metaphysics), and it put me into a total funk. What did it mean? Suddenly, from a world of slow attrition I was erupted into a world of complete replaceability and complete equality. I no longer had any choice in deciding at what subtle point my thoughts crossed over from visibility into nullity's realm. Nullity was now a precipice. When and if I decided not to replace the tape, at that point was I suddenly thrust into the void. Suddenly the world seemed to be enormously at risk. I actually sought to avoid depression by not typing at all. But this upset my wife and children. So I type, but my thoughts are looser, more trivial, less probing. I do not wish to commit my real thoughts to so dangerous an enterprise. And I am thinking, perhaps desperately. For example, although it is true that my words now all have equal clarity, what of the machine itself? Is there not an attrition there? I do not yet have to turn in the entire machine with each ribbon. My scheme of life can still work, only on a larger, longer scale. For my machine, like my ribbon of old, must *eventually* be traded in. But if I choose not to, if I choose with an ailing machine to continue to type on the pristine tapes, might not my old rebelliousness still have scope, the machine producing more and more impressions of pristine nothings, some unsacred cuneiform? And what of my body itself? Is it not, too, wearing away each day, each moment? Will it not, eventually, produce degrees of nothing, if not traded in? Indeed, I think so. My entropic universe is still there. Civilization still struggles, in ever minute degrees, towards nullity. I breathed a whisper (but only a whisper) of joy. The other day, my wife asked me, casually, I think, "And what have you typed today?" and I answered, "My fingers are weak, or weaker, I should say. Have you noticed?" "Yes," she said, with a sad smile, "I have noticed." "The world," I said, "goes on, doesn't it?" "Yes, it goes on," she said. I had the impression she wanted to say more, that perhaps she saw things differently. But she said nothing. Unlike me, she does not type at all. I'm not exactly sure what she does do, only that whatever it is, she's been doing it for over twenty years in my presence, quietly. To some people, that might seem strange. Her name is Josie. But I sometimes call her Josephine, although in fact "Josephine" is recorded on no document. I cannot explain that. In fact, I'm not sure what I can (or should) explain anymore. Next year there *might* well be another "machine," and I shall have to reconstitute the universe. There might not be any such accommodation as was possible this year. Josie will be older. Josie might be dead. If that were to happen, I think I should dig up my old machine, with its old ribbon, and begin to rewrite the history of the world in invisible script. And I should do this forever. Perhaps it is what I have been doing all along without knowing it.

Observations:

1.	My first description is not accurate. There is a diminution of imprint only with each run-through of the ribbon. Within each run-through there is an equality of diminution, so to speak, unless one is considering the greater frequency of certain letters over others within any run-through and hence, actually, an unevenness of diminution because of the greater wear on particular typefaces. At the moment, I do not know how to factor this in. (Why am I such a victim of equations?)

2.	Nullity might not be quite the word for the end product of persistent, even demonic, use of the same ribbon. To be sure, at first there would be fainter impressions yielding gradually to what appeared to be no impression. But then, in a matter of time, the ribbon would become shredded and cease to function on its spools. I would be typing on the bare roller, over and over again. What sort of scroll would this become? What hieroglyphics? And what is the metaphorical content of the shredded ribbon? Am I still dealing with a typewriter? What daredevilish (and foolish) man first called it a typewriter? Could I not type on a pile of junk? Or even on the earth itself? Is nullity really possible?

3.	I cannot pinpoint the time or circumstance when I first called my wife by her non-name Josephine, but I feel it is important to do so. That a non-name should loom so large disturbs me. I feel as if standing on a very thin sheet of ice over a great depth, with no lines to aid me ashore should the ice crack. Why have I ventured there? Still further, there are obviously more non-names than names. At what rate do they enter the world and why? If the world of man ends soon, most of the non-names will never be expressed. Will they cease to exist? Or will the realm of non-names simply signify that our world of piddling names has expired and go its own way? How much more powerful is Josephine than Josie. And how many worlds impend on unspoken discourse.

4.  "Our finite life force." This indeed is the capital with which we empower our constitutions of reality. But there is never any capital improvement: it is always a bad investment. Is there any alternative? I don't know.

5.  "Who can discriminate the degrees of invisibility?" No one, I imply. But is any degree of invisibility life? Perhaps an earlier question—when does invisibility begin? Impossible to say. Is death invisibility? Also difficult to say. (Think about mad Ahab's whale.)

6.  What, actually, is script? Script is always written in blood,

and there is only so much. Then a body dies, and new script is written over old script. I am already a palimpsest. Countless hands, even claws, clutch at my heart. In all this, how can I claim to love? How dare I weep at death? My only respite is in "Josephine" and in uttering it rarely and only with the greatest reverence.

7.   "Nullity was now a precipice." What isn't? The world changes only in ways that do not matter. Yet that *not mattering* is everything. I am content to pin my life there like the tail of the donkey. Here, ten thousand died. And there, what a tragedy we have remembered. Yet something stirs in me I cannot explain. Josie has told me something. It is a script of terrible pain, of loss, despair. If I cry, do my tears reach back eons? What is this Josie? And if Josie dies, can I make do with Josephine, if Josephine be there at all?

8.   "My scheme of life." My scheme of life is to make turtle tracks.

8A.   In all this (pronouns are indeed endearing and wonderful) I can see hints of some vast anthropology, or should it be archeology—or some other word? We beat upward and downward at the same time, and between the two there must be a laughter, if only we could hear it.

8B. "To increase the striking pressure on the keyboard." It is usually possible to offset the inevitable decline of existence by applying more pressure. But only up to a point. There is always that moment when the raw material is insufficient to fuel the needed pressure and decline edges ahead. That moment, surely, is one of life's awful realizations. Wiliness ensues, then philosophy, then death. Thus, "to increase the striking pressure" is comforting but ultimately deluding. It is best to know this and play accordingly.

8C. "Recording some of my choice thoughts." It is only at a very late stage (of *what*?) that the "some" leaps out of me. Why not all? Surely there are not too many. What arcane editorial process chooses some and not others? Perhaps I should spend the rest of my life mulling over those not chosen. Perhaps *they are* my life. But if so, what is the rest? A choice thought: we spend our earthly span editorializing our lives away. But when our editorializing selves die, what happens to the other? What death does it die? What legacy? Is this too steep a brink?

9. Josie, with a sad smile, says, "I have noticed." But noticed what? Surely not just my weakening fingers. She has not told me

what she has noticed. She has mastered a silence of sorts, but not absence. I feel Josie *with* me all the time. And I know that, even were there time, she would not tell me all the things she has noticed. Her silence is like a sun. Can I bear to bask in it? If I scream, will that sun absorb it? I can still grasp her hand, feel its odd unsymmetries, sense her hot blood flowing there. Can that possibly be enough? Can that possibly be all?

## THE MAN IN THE STRETCHER

Now we come to the man in the stretcher again. He has a thing about young Oriental girls. Eventually, in the Alps, snow all around him, there will be revelation. But right now he is sweating somewhere below the middle of Italy. It is summer. He has survived the pestilential marshes of southernmost Italy after debarking from the trireme. As he is rowed ashore there are horn blasts from the ship. The slaves shout in unison. Exactly what they say is not clear, but it is evidently a sign of respect, a tribute. On shore the villagers run to and fro in fear and consternation. They gabble and gobble. Rumor swells and spreads. Already, as he is made comfortable in his World War I stretcher, fantastic tales of him are whispered two hundred miles to the north. Mothers hide young virgins and mature men become impotent. His entourage numbers now about a dozen. Two men always carry the stretcher. Several pull a cart laden with food and supplies. Sometimes there is a donkey. The others walk. It is tough-going through some of the marshes. They sink in, stick, get wet, fall. But there are good moments, too, like the gorging on eels as the fire burns brightly through the night. On occasion he holds up his hand. They stop whatever they are doing, they listen.

"*Mangiate, mangiate,*" he says. He has picked up a little of the language. "*Fate l'amour, ripossatevi, dormite, baciatemi i piedi.*" Make love. Rest. Sleep. Kiss my feet. His voice is deep and gentle. They love him. But they fear him, too. For sometimes his voice is harsh and agitated. They feel his sense of urgency, his despair, his anger. They know about the Oriental girl, but they never speak of it. Sometimes he asks Philoma, the most beautiful of them, to dance for him. She is large and shapely. Her clothes are diaphanous. She has a large mouth and magnificent teeth. As she dances her large nipples harden and show through. Sweat pours from her face. The entourage make what music they can from odds and ends. Faster, always faster, to some final point, always indefinable. The man in the stretcher's eyes glisten. And then, when all is suddenly still and silent, a few tears squeeze out. He signals them to move on. They pick up. They begin to move. Philoma strips quickly. Someone dumps a pail of water over her. She puts on fresh clothing. And they are gone. One hears only soft flute sounds. The place they have left is somehow sacred, and for months afterwards the young lovers of the villages will make love there.

The place where he is sweating is a land of rubble. Tin cans, ashes, old bricks, holes with ooze, shrubs, thorns, some patches of grass. It is like the skin of a festering and mangy dog.

In the distance to one side, the outline of a city. Dozens of smokestacks rise into the sky. To the other side, hills. The city is not on their path, and they veer off. A figure comes toward them from the city. She is running, and sometimes she falls. She waves to them and yells, *Aspetti!* They do not stop. But at last she reaches them. She is bleeding, dirty, exhausted. Her dress is torn. She smells. They still do not stop. They pay no attention to her. Her name is Wanda. She wants the help of the man in the stretcher. She is fat, ugly, stupid. Her face is scarred, her teeth are rotten. But she wants love, she wants children, she feels the same things that beautiful women feel. Inside, she says, she is tender and loving, clean, she has a soul. Can he help her? Will he? She keeps falling down as she is talking, getting more bloody. Her voice is raw, tears stream from her eyes. The man in the stretcher holds up his hand. They stop. They put him down. They look at her. He tells her to take off her clothes. She hesitates. He signals his carriers to move on. She screams no and takes off her dress. Everything, he says. Tutti. She takes off everything. Naked she is even worse than before. She is enormous. Her breasts rest heavily on her great fat belly which folds over to hide her corner of love. Thick hair juts out from her armpits. Her soul is not visible. However, her ankles are small. They are her best feature. She is sweating profusely, and some hold their noses as they smile. "Kneel down," he says. She does. "Close your eyes. Recite one hundred Hail Marys. Do not rush." As she begins to murmur, he signals. They pick him up and silently move off. Soon they are mounting the hills. In the distance the fat figure still prays. A few dogs have wandered by, sniffed, and left. Near her are other figures. Stunted, ugly men. They have come up out of the rubble. They are curious. The kneeling figure arouses them. They close in on her and drop their pants. When she is done, she opens her eyes and sees the men. She is frightened and tries to scream, but she cannot. They get on her, one after another. As her head twists and jerks she sees the man in the stretcher off in the hills. Her voice returns, and she screams curses at him. Son of a pig! Man with a head of excrement! *Figlio di puttana!* Dog diddler! Defiler of virgins! Ah! Ah! Ahhh! The echoes reach him, and he raises his hand in benediction. She has men, she has love. In time she will have children. He is satisfied.

  The first villages they walked through were silent. Even the babies were silent. The man in the stretcher did not even look at them. The flies and mosquitoes took all his attention. Occasionally he whips his carriers. They exert themselves more. Several others walk near him and kill insects. One fans him. Sometimes he is able to read. And of course he has correspondence and notes. One man carries what he has already written. He is his secretary and general man of affairs. His name is Armond. He is in love with Philoma, but she will not let him touch her

## The Man in the Stretcher

except to rub oils when she is weary. Then she lies naked and lets him stroke her. It is amusing to the others. He strokes her very well. He is an educated man. He dribbles at the mouth. There will be time to talk of them and others later. In the marshes they chance upon a raft. With some small adjustments it will be serviceable and save them much difficult traveling. They push off with long poles. There is no sun. In the still water the land and all that is on it is reflected dimly. They do not talk. One of the entourage, an Iranian or Greek with no name, dips his pole too deep and is pulled off the raft when it sticks. He screams for help in his native tongue. But no one understands what he is saying. The man in the stretcher tosses crusts of bread on the water. "*Pane!*" he calls. "*Pane!*" They move on. When the bread reaches the pole, the man is gone. Fish snap up at the bread, leaving small whirlpools. Soon there is mist all around. And music. In the village ahead there is a procession. The children of the village sing in trembling soprano voices. They carry flowers and statues. Some of the men wear large grotesque masks of fish. The young women blush, and the old women murmur prayers into their black shawls. Six men carry a gilded catafalque in which a nude girl sits before burning incense. Their priest, holding a long thin knife, leads them to the water. The mist enshrouds everything. The priest holds up his hands. All are silent. Then, from the mist, the man in the stretcher speaks in a deep voice. "*Salve, piscatores! Salve, pis-*

*catores! Salve, piscatores!*" The raft comes briefly into view. It floats by. They look at one another. The secretary is typing. The horns of the trireme sound. The mist covers everything. The water is colored red.

When next we see the raft it is coming out from under a bridge. Again the horns of the trireme sound. Now there is sun. People stroll by the river. It is a day of rest in the city. The man in the stretcher holds a staff with an eagle and wears the helmet of a centurion. The strolling people look in disbelief. For a moment they feel fear. A small boat capsizes when everyone rushes to one side to embark. As they climb the stairs people are already gathering. They push, they stumble. Knees bleed. One old man is dumped into the river, but no one has any time for him. "Barbarians!" he cries. He drowns very quickly. The man in the stretcher and his entourage move off. Only a white-haired lady with a cane remains, looking at the river. "Curiosity killed a cat!" she screams. She spits and hobbles after the crowd. There is no hope that she will catch up with them. Already they have reached a main thoroughfare. Several hundred people surround them, with more coming every moment. They move out into the traffic. Cars swerve and hit one another. People are run over, fruit stands overturned. Everything piles up. Curses are everywhere. Hundreds of horns are blowing. But those who can walk follow the man in the stretcher. They want to see what he is going to do. Soon all the roads are blocked with wrecks. Sirens scream. Whistles blow. Policemen run to and fro. The man in the stretcher moves on until he reaches the central square. There, thousands are gathered. Their heads are turned up. A few are kneeling. They are listening to a speaker. But the man in the stretcher disrupts their concentration. He takes out his whip and whips his carriers, and some of the listeners as well. "*Vite, vite!*" he shrieks. A path through the crowd opens for them. Almost running they reach a wall beyond which they cannot go. His carriers look at him. "*Basta!*" he says, and signals them to lift him. They take him to the wall, where he undoes his pants and relieves himself. Then he turns to the crowd, smiles, laughs just a little self-consciously, holds up his hand in blessing, and cries out, "*Bene! Bene!*" The crowd at first does not know what to do. The carriers put him on his stretcher. They move off, slowly at first, then more quickly, the man in the stretcher bestowing vague benedictions. Fruit, cabbages, eggplants fly through the air. The crowd laughs. The entourage runs. Some of their clothes are ripped off. The crowd curses and pursues them. The square is empty but for the litter. Pigeons swoop in. The speaker drones on. Meanwhile the entourage has dashed into a narrow alley. Men appear on the rooftops, throwing stones at them as they pass. Then they urinate on them and laugh. As they laugh, the ones behind them crowd forward to see, pushing them off. They break their bones, they break their necks. The people pursuing the entourage run over them, some stumbling and falling. Soon the alley is impossible to pass through because of the bodies. Everyone is shrieking. An ambulance pulls up at the edge of the bodies. The driver and attendant get out with a stretcher and look. Then they get back in and drive away. The entourage escapes. Back in the square, the old lady is going as fast as she can, swinging her cane at the pigeons in her way and cursing. The speaker continues. "The old fool is dead!" she shouts. "*Morto!*" Then, "Pray for him!" She cries and hurries on.

The next scene is a brief one. It is by the seashore. Small waves break on a clean beach behind which are steep cliffs. The sounds of sea birds as they fly from the cliff and skirt over the water. The man in the stretcher, fully clothed, is sitting in the water. Some of his entourage are with him. The others are on the sand or climbing the cliffs. They are licking their wounds, washing, resting. Philoma flirts as she bathes. The sun is shining. They are happy. The man in the stretcher is staring out into the ocean. He speaks. "*Acqua,*" he says. He is learning the language. "*Acqua! Acqua...*" And as he speaks he lifts up his arms and lets the water trickle down. Horn sounds from the trireme far at sea. He claps his hands to depart. One of his entourage runs up to him excitedly with a speckled egg from the cliff. They all stare at it in wonder. The man in the stretcher places it gently on the water. It floats. The entourage gasps in astonishment. It floats away. He signals. The carriers lift up the stretcher, which he has been sitting on, and march down the beach, some gamboling to flute sounds. This is the scene of the miracle of the floating egg.

    It is now time to introduce the members of the entourage. Philoma of course is already known. There is more to say about her, but it can wait. What about the man in the stretcher? He was originally found in the North African desert by his carriers, Heintz and Ruffo, and Philoma. Heintz has deserted from the French Foreign Legion. Ruffo is a former eunuch in a sultan's harem. They meet in a filthy Arab village and decide to team up. But before they can leave, the Sultan passes through. From the edge of the crowd, Ruffo recognizes one of the girls. It is Philoma. She sees him and pleads with her eyes. That night, he goes to the Sultan's tents, kills three of the Sultan's guards, and escapes with Philoma, who is the Sultan's plum. Heintz is angry but attracted to Philoma. They steal two camels and leave in darkness just before the Sultan's horsemen gallop through the village cutting off heads. When the sun is overhead, they are in the middle of the desert. They are hot, thirsty, and lost. Philoma insists on riding with Ruffo instead of Heintz, even though Ruffo is nearly 400 pounds. Their camel soon dies. The three of them argue, and Heintz's camel runs off. They then walk. They are ready to die of thirst and exposure when they see the man in the stretcher. He is sitting on the stretcher on the sand. They come up to him and for a long time they stare at him. Is he a mirage? Have they become struck by the sun? They touch him. They confer. Then they argue again. Heintz wants to kill him. Philoma calls him a fool and wants to know what good that will do. Ruffo says they can drink his blood. Then the man in the stretcher makes signals. He points to Philoma and then to Heintz. He jabs the fist of one hand into the palm of the other several times quickly. They all understand but do nothing. The man in the stretcher jabs again, more insistently this time with sounds from his throat. Heintz grabs Philoma, throws her down, and makes love to her. Ruffo sits on the sand by their feet and cries. When they are done, the man on the stretcher snaps his whip and they pick up his stretcher. Philoma mutters that she does not like making love on sand. Within an hour they sight the sea and a small city on a bay. This episode is known as the meeting in the desert.

    The city by the sea is as dirty as the village, but it is larger. They stop at the first bistro and go in, leaving the man in the stretcher in the street amidst camel dung. Children gather round. He gives them coins, and they provide shade and keep the flies off him. Inside, Philoma dances for the Arabs, whose long tongues flicker in and out and around their lips. She is a juicy morsel. They throw coins. Heintz and Ruffo pick them up. A small European man tries to hide one with his foot, and Heintz and Ruffo throw him into the street. Then they buy drinks, get

### The Man in the Stretcher

drunk, and come out staggering. The man in the stretcher whips them. They pick up the stretcher and head for the docks. Philoma follows. And the European man, whose name is Armond and who will become secretary to the man in the stretcher. These are the North African disciples. When they reach the docks the trireme comes in quickly, the horn sounding and the rowing rhythm beat out loud and fast. The oars hold, the trireme glides smoothly around, the oars are pulled in, and as it touches the stone wall, a gangway is thrown over and a carpet rolled over it. The man in the stretcher is carried aboard, the gangway withdrawn, the ship drifts off, and the oars begin to pull. The fighting men of the ship are lined up. The man in the stretcher and his entourage walk past them, in review, to the master of the ship. He sits on a throne, fat, debauched, and unsmiling. Then he snaps his fingers, and female slaves bring out huge trays of fruit, roast pig, a calf, a dozen sheeps' heads on a pole, and wine. "*Mangiate. Mangiate,*" he says. He and the man in the stretcher laugh suddenly. As the trireme disappears in the distance, the horn sounds again. On the dock an Arab picks up a piece of silk material from Philoma's attire. He smells it and smiles. Another Arab grabs it, smells it, smiles, and rubs it between his legs. An argument ensues. Soon thirty men are fighting. The trireme horn sounds again. The African continent is left behind.

And now, what about the man in the stretcher? Who is he?

What does he look like? Well, he is clean shaven usually. He looks like a businessman, perhaps an accountant. He is of medium height, about twenty pounds too heavy, more meticulous than not about his clothing, although he seldom changes it. He seldom smiles, talks less, never stands on his feet. His teeth are rotten. Perhaps that is why he seldom smiles. Periodically he relieves himself. Sometimes he writes as he is being carried, sometimes he dictates to his secretary, but no one ever hears what he dictates. Nothing is known about his past. He has always existed on the stretcher. No one has ever seen his legs. Only one thing about him stands out—his special concern for young Oriental girls. That is clearly the object of his quest. Why he searches in Italy is obscure. But there is no doubt that he sometimes feels very close to success. His urgency at those moments infects everyone. The pace quickens. Hearts beat faster. Eyes dart like eagles in the sky. But thus far success has eluded him. There has been no conspicuous Oriental migration to Italy. There is some suspicion that he is Italian, but he speaks the language only haltingly. He has no moustache. His chest appears to be hairy (as do his arms), and sometimes he has erections. He eats little most of the time, but on occasion, as with the Feast of the Eels, he gorges himself. His relationship with his entourage is remote but absolute. They all understand that if necessary they will die for him. It is possible that Philoma provides special services for him, but there is no proof. He sleeps soundly, sweats a good deal, and can nap in a sitting position. His integrity is total. No one has ever questioned it. He has performed miracles, but they are of minor interest to him. His ears are delicately formed. His eyebrows are bushy. His eyes are blue. Usually he sits straight-backed in his stretcher, but sometimes he has pillows and lounges, eating figs, olives, or grapes. For a brief period he had a monkey and seemed amused and diverted by it. But it disappeared one night, and, although the morning departure was conspicuously delayed, he never alluded to it. Whenever possible he drinks goat milk. He feels it is the nectar of life. No doubt he is preparing himself in some mysterious way for his Oriental beauty. He appears at times to be meditating. Frequently he fixes his position by staring at the sun. Sometimes he barks out changes in direction, some of them incomprehensible. "Right! Right! Quickly! Now left! More! Right again! *Diagonale! Diagonale!* Good! Armond!" And then he dictates. Even when there is fog he peers upwards, as if for the sun. But on the whole, they make less distance in fog. He has no control over the elements, but he is impervious to them except that he sweats a lot. He has made them travel whole days in drenching rain. Once, when he detected some grumbling, he commanded them all to strip naked and roll up their clothes. They became filthy with mud. In that manner they passed through a small town. A man looking out the window of a cafe said there was a group of naked people passing by and was laughed at. The few old women and children they met in the street crossed themselves. A dog howled. For a few minutes they trailed a funeral procession, which made the mourners run to the cemetery as fast as dignity and the occasion would allow. Just before they left the town a postman came up and delivered a letter to the man in the stretcher. He ripped it open, threw away the insides, and told Armond to put the envelope and stamps in with his Near Eastern collection. He appears to get pleasure from simple things—combing his hair, picking his ears and nose, blowing his nose, spitting, airing his feet, farting, belching, scratching, shaving en route, cutting his nails, and looking down his pants. He sees none of these activities as indecorous, nor does anyone else in his circle. He wears a charm around his neck which he received from a sailor on the trireme, the fifth man to join his entourage. But since he spoke no known language and was drowned soon after their arrival on the peninsula there is no need to speak of him further. Word has somehow preceded the arrival of the trireme, for several people are waiting on shore to join the man in the stretcher. Among them are a group of acrobats variously related. A certain Garibaldi is ostensibly the half-brother of Garibalda. They had the same father, but his mother was Garibalda's half-sister, making him her nephew also. He may also be her father because as an adolescent, before Garibalda was born, he slept often with his mother's sister, that is, his father's wife. Garibalda's mother was also her sister's mother, but her sister's father was a gypsy of great fame in Romania. They are also married and have two grown children, a daughter with small buttocks and large breasts who often uses a single crutch. She, too, is an acrobat. Her name is La Pequeña. Her brother is named Chico. The four of them, or the six or eight of them, are constantly bickering, and something in all this gives the man in the stretcher a deep satisfaction. They also juggle. Several of the people who join them upon debarkation later drop away and are replaced by others. Notable among them is a Sicilian transvestite known as Rose of England because he can say, "I speek Engleesh vairy good." He is very unhappy and dresses shabbily. He has a tragic history and wears lipstick like a wound. The man in the stretcher tapped his pen on the frame of his stretcher and in monotone uttered, "*Bravo. Magnifique.*" Rose was deliriously happy. But that night, his face in ruin, he sat apart in deep depression. For a brief time there was speculation that Rose of England was related to the man in the stretcher. The strongest support for this, oddly enough, is that among all the fictions Rose has recited about himself the one most believed is that Rose was once a goatherd. The man in the stretcher never acknowledges any relationship, but it is indisputable that no one but Rose ever milks the goats that provide him with his nectar of life. This and these, then, are the most specific things known about the man in the stretcher. No doubt more will be revealed inadvertently and by indirection. And in his actions his being is ever more defined. Small nagging questions will always remain. Does he have tattoos, birthmarks, pimples? Is he circumcised? (He *appears* to be, but Heintz and Ruffo are very close-mouthed about it). Does he, and when and where, wash his private parts? Is he possibly an Arab? Was he in the War? Who was his mother? Does he have political convictions? (Is he a Communist?) How did his teeth get so rotten? How many days was he in the desert? Does the amulet around his neck give him power? What will happen when he finds his Oriental beauty? And why doesn't he go to China? But by and large these are quibbles. What is clearly known is that he has power. He holds his entourage in the palm of his hand. Further, he knows where he is going; he has a sense of personal *destiny*. Finally, he is obviously *holy*, but in ways impossible to understand. The others in the entourage need not be described here, only named. They were Rachel, Ethan, the woman who nursed her baby, Papalucci (the cook), a dwarf, an idiot. From time to time, as has been indicated, there are hangers-on.

In the next scene the entourage is obviously older and more worn out. They are feeling the strain of the quest. There is a sense of the seasons rotating. They wear more clothing. Slyly they bring nubile Italian girls into the presence of the man in the stretcher. They hope he will succumb. Usually he pretends not to notice. When he does notice, he feels them in the back, the buttocks, and says, "*Grossa. Troppa grossa*," no matter how thin they are. One night they make large Oriental masks and put on a dumb show for him in front of a large fire. Garibaldi narrates. "It is the harem of an Oriental potentate," he says. "The young girls are lounging, waiting for their lord and master. A eunuch stands guard. The potentate enters after a hard day of work. 'Dance,' he says, 'Dance for me.' He lies back on scented pillows, and his harem dances. Listen. Can you hear the music? The dance begins delicately. These girls are the flower of the Orient. But as the drums come to dominate, the dance becomes more frenzied, more physical. One of the girls stands out from the others, and finally she alone is dancing. The music reaches a climax, and she stops. The potentate has been aroused. He beckons to her. She comes and kneels by his side. And then he speaks." Here Garibaldi ceases his narration, and the potentate, played by the dwarf, speaks in a dummy's voice, "Where have you been all my life?" he says, as he removes the mask from Philoma. "*Basta!*" screams the man in the stretcher. "*Basta!*" He cracks the whip. "*Avanti! Avanti!*" And although they had expected to be settled for the night, they pick up and go, some still with their masks on. The darkness is all around them, and thick woods. Strange animals make sounds as they pass. Sometimes it seems as if some gigantic creature is rushing at them from the darkness. "*Basta!*" screams the man in the stretcher at the darkness. And, whatever it was, it ceases. Nevertheless, the entourage cringes and cowers. They are frightened. And when a pack of thirty snarling dogs block their passage, they drop the man in the stretcher and run. The dogs advance on him, their mouths dripping with saliva, their eyes bloodshot, low growls in their throats. They are all around him, within inches. Suddenly he screams again, "*Basta!*" and the dogs scatter, yelping, their tails between their legs. "*Avanti! Avanti!*" he calls out to his entourage, and they return, looking sheepish. As they continue, a few of the dogs join them. Soon they are out of the woods. They enter a town in the center of which a rally is being held. Several men sit on the platform in the center of town. A speaker is rousing the crowd with talk of injustice, slavery, and a new dawn. They are all prostitutes instead of free men. They look down into the muck instead of upwards into the sun. Instead of circling quietly around the crowd, the man in the stretcher cuts right through it to the platform. The nursing mother is on the donkey with the idiot behind her. The dwarf, who still wears his mask, leads the goat. Ethan begins to beat a drum. The crowd gives way, the speaker hesitates, then stops and confers with the other men on the platform. They think it is a trick of the opposition and are about to denounce them. But the crowd is behaving peculiarly. Women are kissing the clothes of the nursing mother. The idiot is blessing the crowd. People cross themselves. A few get on their knees. The speaker decides to wait, to play it safe. He welcomes the procession as if it were part of his act. He hugs the man in the stretcher (who spits) as if he is a wounded war hero. Someone finds a medal to pin on him. The man in the stretcher takes the microphone and speaks amidst the frequent cheers. "Pasta-eaters of Italy," he says. "I have come to save you." He beckons to Armond, who brings him one of his notebooks, from which he reads excerpts. As he reads, the acrobats do clumsy tumbling tricks. Ethan rolls the drum for them. La Pequeña wears a tight weightlifter's suit under her cape (which she has flung off magnificently), has difficulty keeping both her enormous breasts inside. Every time she moves, one or another pops out the side. Sometimes, as when she bows, both come out. But she keeps pushing them back in, she keeps smiling, even though her crutch is a nuisance. The crowd is in agony of confusion and excitement. "This land is under a curse!" proclaims the man in the stretcher. He flicks the pages. "Only last year," he continues, "the silt in the canals of Venice rose three inches. Venice is sinking into the sea. Diseased crustaceans nibble at the foundations of the palaces of the Doges. On the beaches everywhere, rats! Already they are marrying into the lower classes. Look around you at the rat people. Yes, even here. The Italian people are no longer pure. They are choking on their pasta. In Roma, in Genoa, in Milan, in Napoli. No longer do Italians sing happily. Babies are born yellow. They do not cry; they croak. Their mother's milk is sour. Breasts hang thin and loose. Women everywhere are dying giving birth to homunculi! Where are the peasants and haystacks of yesteryear? Look at your teeth. Vitamin E! Vitamin K1, K2, K3! Your teeth are gnawing at the very foundations of your greatness and your glory! Look to the ache in your groin!—And the tides! Every morning they come sweeping in, bringing dead bodies, tin cans, cantaloupes—mother, father, daughter, cousin, village priest, pet dogs and cats. *Canaries!*" As he speaks, the crowd nods assent. They mutter, "*Si. Si.* He is right. Why only last week my cousin..." and hold their crotches at La Pequeña's breasts, which are truly huge, with large brown cupcake nipples. A few people weep. They are all caught into the rhythm of the man in the stretcher. Each statement is a thunderbolt, each word transfixes them. "You step willingly on the lime twig and wait only to have your necks pinched. You make love on the bones of the past and spew babies into the garbage of the present. *O mama mia!* Tomorrow you will die! Wheat futures are dim! Tourism is rampant! Cash in your stocks! Destroy your grapes! Vomit! Vomit! Before it is too late!" He snaps his fingers at the tumblers. They stop. La Pequeña hobbles over to him. He tucks in her breasts, puts on her cape. "*Basta*," he says. They proceed to leave at once. The other speakers on the platform bow respectfully. Someone gives the man in the stretcher a bag of fruit and vegetables, and as

## The Man in the Stretcher

he is carried through the now mostly kneeling throng he crushes tomatoes, zucchini, eggplant on their heads in blessing. "Cut off your testicles!" he says. "You will die tomorrow! You are a freak! You will never bear children! You have cancerous worms in your brain!" Soon he is gone, and the crowd is immobile in silence. Then, from the dark, his voice. "Pasta-eaters of Italy! Destroy your city! Burn it to the ground! Impoverish yourselves! Then the voice drifts off. "*Spaghetti!... Pasta fazoola!... Pizza!... Mama mia!... O sole mio!...*" Again there is silence. Then, suddenly released from their spell, the people of the town go insane and burn the town to the ground. The next morning, the militia moves in. Weary people sit disconsolately in ditches by the road, patching their wounds. When asked what has happened, they answer without conviction that they are going to Jerusalem to kill the infidel. As the soldiers scratch their heads a few people of the town laugh. Then more. Then all. The soldiers think the whole town is mad. But they were not there. They did not see the breasts of Pequeña. They did not hear the man in the stretcher speak. Even so, at last they laugh too.

    Somewhere on this pilgrimage there should be a love story. And it seems it should be about Philoma and—Ah, but that is most certainly the question. With Heintz? Ruffo? Armond? The man in the stretcher. Even the mysterious Ethan? Or possibly Rose of England? Anyone is possible. Whom will Philoma, goddess of love, love. Philoma is always making love. When she walks, she makes love. When she sleeps, the earth receives her body with lust. When she bathes the very water becomes orgasmic. See how her breasts float, how the nipples stiffen with pleasure. See how her pubic hairs nest cunningly on the water like some cozy sea urchin. When she swims, the whole ocean is made ready for love. But whom shall she love? It is already known that she has loved a sultan and loved Heintz. But the former she could not help, and the latter was a command of the man in the stretcher. How else could he have pacified the three of them and got himself removed from the desert? What Philoma decides is that the three leading contenders shall compete for her favor. There will be a night of contest. Philoma begins by reaching under her dress and pulling off her red undergarment. She holds it aloft, a banner. Everyone cheers. The goddess of love is ready to receive her suitors. Heintz is the first. He is dressed as a first *danceur*. He wears black tights and a ruffled white blouse with flowing sleeves. But he bulges too much, there is no sleekness. Clearly he is nervous. The music begins. Somewhere they have acquired a gypsy violinist (Yes, it is possibly Garibalda's sister's father. The journey is full of strange coincidences). He plays music from *Les Sylphides*, *A Midsummer's Night's Dream*, *The Nutcracker Suite*, *Swan Lake*. Heintz stands on his toes, runs with small quick steps, leaps, twists, holds his fingers in the air. When the music is fast he does an awkward jig. During the adagios he moves like a drunken hippopotamus. He is totally without grace, and everyone laughs. But his face, even twisted in frustration, has never looked more beautiful, more spiritual. When he is done he walks off and sulks in the shadows. Armond is next. He is dressed like a weightlifter, an acrobat, an aerialist. The drum rolls. He comes on doing cartwheels and falls on his head. He attempts to stand on his hands and falls on his back. Then come the weights. They are enormous. He seems intimidated. He looks at Philoma, she rubs her breasts, he walks up to the weights, bends, and pulls. Nothing happens. Howls of laughter. He pulls more. Nothing happens. The laughter swells. Now he is pulling with all his strength. He holds nothing back. He turns white, then blue. His eyes bulge. The laughter stops. Dead silence as Armond pulls. Everyone realizes that he will not give up. The whole world is Armond pulls. Everyone is pulling with Armond. There is a great communal straining and grunting. Then there is a sudden tear of pain across his face. Something has given way. He shrivels, clutches his groin, and begins to tremble and sweat. Finally Garibaldi and Chico carry him off amidst applause. Philoma shrugs sadly, purses her lips, and kisses the air. It was a good try. Ruffo is last. He is dressed as the complete lover. He is Romeo, Cassanova, and Lord Byron all rolled into one. He struts up and down like a peacock rolling his eyes at the women, who twitter and giggle. Now he thrusts his buttocks at them, now his hips. Someone crows like a rooster. Someone hands him a mandolin. He sings a love song like a lizard. The women dart their tongues at him and howl. His song done, he struts before Philoma, seated on a throne. "I am the cock of the walk!" he says and darts his tongue at Philoma, as someone crows again. He gets on his hands and knees in front of her. "I am irresistible! I drive women mad!" he says, wiggling his buttocks and darting his tongue. The entourage is in hysterics. Advancing toward Philoma he says, "I can unlock any treasure chest!" and darts his tongue. Philoma's eyes glisten. She rolls her tongue around her lips and slowly spreads her legs. "*Avanti!* scream the entourage. "*Avanti!*" And Ruffo gallops into the darkness of Philoma's legs as she gives forth a scream of pleasure and throws her red undergarment into the air, where for a brief moment, the brilliant red on a perfect black, it is suspended. When it falls, ever so slowly, everyone is peacefully asleep except the man in the stretcher, whose eyes are blazing, and two dogs making love. One odd detail: Armond sleeps with La Pequña's nipple in his mouth.

    The next morning they wake up from the cold. Wind is blowing across them. The horn from the trireme sounds. Everyone feels the urgency, and without any prompting they pack up quickly and leave. The man in the stretcher wears a heavy sweater and muffler. He brushes the falling leaves away from him angrily.

They have a long straight stretch and they take it at a trot. Armond brings him tea, and although he spills most of it he mutters, "*Bene.*" Then Armond takes some dictation. A little further on, the *carabinieri* are shooting it out with some bandits in a farmhouse. The entourage hesitates. The man in the stretcher snaps his fingers. Flute, fiddle, and drum music. The shooting lets up. The entourage bend their heads and rush through, saying, "*Scusi. Scusi,*" smiling to the right and to the left. The *carabinieri* are so dumbstruck they do not see the bandits join the entourage, and when it is out of sight they resume their shooting. Later the bandits leave, except for one, who joins the entourage. They are profuse in their thanks and leave cheese and wine. By noon the entourage is crossing upland meadows. Far off, the sea is barely visible, and there is the echo of the trireme horn. The clouds are low. On a balcony of a remote Alpine cottage a man stretches and utters, "What a relief to be away from it all" just as the entourage scurries by, waving, dumping their garbage, breaking their wine bottles, Rose of England blowing him a kiss. Mid-afternoon they rest on a ledge. They are exhausted. As they are eating, three mountain climbers climb up to their ledge, stare at them in disbelief, for there is no path, and climb the face above them. Soon it begins to snow. A strange smile crosses the face of the man in the stretcher. "*Vite,*" he says softly. "*Vite.*" They set off at once in blinding snow. Later, the mountain climbers look up, and several miles ahead, racing across the snow—the entourage. They decide to turn back. Mystery is afoot. Several hours after that, the man in the stretcher holds up his hand. "*Basta*," he says. They put down their loads. He looks at his carriers and snaps his fingers. Just before he leaves, he addresses the entourage. "We meet no more. Build here a city. I go to the next stage of my journey." Philoma hesitates, then kisses his forehead. He points upward, and they leave. The entourage squats and huddles together to keep warm. The snow continues to fall. It is very thick. No one talks. Time passes. At last Heintz and Ruffo return. They join the others. They point off in the distance to where they have left the man in the stretcher. And there he is, a mile or so further up, sitting in the snow as he once was in the desert. Who will carry him from here? Will anyone? Who carried him into the desert? The snow is quickly covering him. He is staring ahead intently. And then he sees it. Movement. Behind a hummock of snow. Flute trills. It is a small animal, perhaps a rabbit. But no, a head peeks out, first one side, then another, quickly. It is the small pert face of an Oriental girl. She has a mischievous smile, and giggles as she peeks. The man in the stretcher smiles slowly. Then she stands, or rather, pops up. She is naked. Her skin is smooth and pale, her breasts are small but sensuous, her pubic hairs a tuft of filaments. She appears not to feel the cold. With her long hair flowing, she runs crookedly across the snow, towards the man in the stretcher, closer, closer,

## The Man in the Stretcher

always giggling, becoming more and more beautiful and desirable, until she reaches the spot where he is—or was (for he is no longer visible), and keeps on running into the falling snow until she disappears. Then silence. Snow and silence. Nothing more. Nothing.

<u>Addendum</u>:

At this point there is *Fine* across the screen, perhaps the film credits again. It doesn't matter. There is, perhaps, a sense of incompleteness, and for this reason a few program notes would be to the good. For example, the man in the stretcher was never seen again, at least not in Italy. Ethan died of spinal meningitis about eight years later. The acrobats froze to death. I cannot tell you about Philoma. Ruffo returned to his Sultan's harem, where, as punishment, he had his tongue cut out. Heintz became insane. Armond became an obscure clerk in the civil service. Rose of England set up a ménage with a British nobleman and learned to speak English very well. As for the others—who knows? They no doubt ended up as other people do. The events are all based on fact, of course. They did found a city (a village, really) as they were instructed. Not many people find their way there. The bandit who joined them at the end became its first mayor. Perhaps it was through one of his rare visitors that many years later a notebook turned up in Genoa, which, it was purported, once belonged to the man in the stretcher. It was filled with gibberish and was bought by a mysterious Semitic collector, who evidently burned or buried it, for it was never heard of again. As for the child that Wanda so brutally conceived, he became a Prince of the Church and made his mother a very happy woman.

# Afterword: The Man with the Beast in Him

In her illuminating essay on Bertolt Brecht (*Men in Dark Times*, 1968), Hannah Arendt charts Brecht's course from his early pagan writings to his final compelled (as Arendt sees it) obeisance to Stalinism. When Brecht advised us to "embrace the butcher," he meant Stalin, who, mass murderer though he was, was still, according to B.B., a cut above the alternatives: fascism and capitalism.

But long before embracing Stalin, Brecht wrote a not atypical poem, "Chorale of the Man Baal," celebrating the Phoenician idol, king of the castaways, carousers and bestialized underclass. Precisely because of their marginalization, the Baal-worshippers were able to live more intensely and authentically in a tragically finite but fundamentally good world soiled only by the institutions that attempted to strangle it.

The later Marxist Brecht is obviously unlike Kenneth Bernard, but his early Brueghel-like celebrations of peasant saturnalia in the context of a doomed mortality, reminded me of Bernard's writing. Virtually every fiction in *The Man in the Stretcher*, spanning almost forty years, is thematically about death, "awash with mortality," as Bernard puts it in "Losing Ground." The Baal-like bestiality persistently celebrated in these texts amounts finally to a *No in Thunder!* defiantly addressed to death, which will nonetheless in due course undo us all.

Consistent from the beginning in Bernard's fiction, poetry and drama is the professed identification with the untamed, the bestial. "Professed" because as with Kafka and Beckett, with whom Bernard has close affinities, the irony, almost always apparent in the text, is that while the identification with the bestial may be posited, it can never be realized—except as fantasy. Bernard's narrator-protagonist is much too embedded an educated bourgeois to actually tear off his clothes and dance deliriously.

Akin in his distancing irony to Beckett and Kafka, Bernard is different from other writers with similarly untamed presumptions, such as William Burroughs, Ted Hughes, Antonin Artaud, and even Charles Bukowski. Burroughs in his assumed subaltern status as junkie-pederast; Hughes in his assumed status as chthonian Yorkshireman; and Artaud in embracing madness—though each of the three was a refined intellectual like Bernard—strive to merge with the untamed. The prideful, proletarian Bukowski, on the other hand, inhabits that privileged bestialized space as his birthright—especially when he's drunk.

The alienation from the untamed is enforced technically by Bernard's characteristic manner of discourse: an exposition or treatise, often with learned references and mock-footnotes, endnotes or commentaries. Unlike his poetry and drama, where Bernard tends to celebrate bestiality without mediation, or even markers of so-called normalcy, in his fiction, it is the discourse that is front and center, while the drama or "action" is secondary. Where there is dialogue, it is mostly "free indirect discourse," combining actual dialogue with the narrator's mediation. That is, the dialogue is typically "focalized" or reported by the narrator, the invariable "I" who relates the narrative retrospectively and who alone "sees," however unreliably, the action. So too the characterization tends to be focalized through the narrator. The disposition in these fictions is really toward exposition, a highly eccentric, ongoing personal essay.

My point is the seeming oddity of a writer as gifted and resourceful as Bernard (he writes flexibly in three mediums) relying largely if not exclusively on a single model of narration, which in fact is as much exposition as narration. It must be said, however, that the expository model is elastic, and Bernard stretches the fabric in sometimes extraordinary ways, even as Borges (whom some of these fictions recall) stretches his own expository model in unexpected directions.

Regarding Bernard's principal subject: Is his acclaimed untamed ever accessed? And if so, to what effect?

The untamed is in fact accessed on numerous occasions, nearly always fatally or impotently. In "The Man With The Beast in Him," the narrator, alienated himself from the auspicious beast, witnesses its lineaments in the dying features of his friend. What then does he do? "I turned and went to the nearby window. And there, gazing out at a landscape that yet held back the frost, I wept the first true tears in my life since I was a child."

"Child" calls up a related motif, familiar of course in Blake, Wordsworth and the other Romantics, of innocence or, as Bernard calls it, in "Ex Facto Oritur Ius," *transparency*. The eye is transparent at birth but then "reality" sets in and the law takes over with its "discipline and punish." In this fiction, the character appears to live his entire life with the dim hope that one day, perhaps as he is dying, the imposed strictures will collapse and once again, however briefly, he will become *transparent*. The unhappy truth is that the world as constituted will not tolerate untamed passion, unless one is a sociopath or mediates and filters the passion through sport or art, as Bernard himself does as writer.

The single way for an "ordinary" human to access the ecstasy of the untamed, unmediated, is to die for it. As does the East Indian field worker, in "The Third Kiss, or Cobra Woman Meets the Bag Lady," who uncovers a cobra. He is immediately enthralled "even as he loosens his sphincter, loosens everything, fouling the heavy air he was learning to love . . . [He] knows

## The Man in the Stretcher

rather than feels the timeless kiss of cobra, and then the swift paralysis, rooted to the experience, cut off so totally from his world. He knows the smell of cobra, but whom can he tell?"

*After such knowledge what forgiveness?*

Smell, incidentally, is Bernard's narrators' privileged sense, the sense closest to animal. And the smell is always of mortality. If the human manages to get close enough to the bestial to smell it, he has committed an upside-down hubris for which he will suffer and likely die.

I began this discussion by distinguishing Brecht's left politics from Bernard's mostly apolitical fiction. In fact there is a "politics" of compassion functioning in Bernard's texts. The text about cobra (without definite or indefinite article) cited above, is also about "the bag lady," that "bundled figure in the doorway," who has been so isolated and degraded that in her bestialized status, her putrefaction, she has an affinity with cobra—without however partaking of the ecstasy.

The writer's compassion for the outcast of one stripe or other, human and animal, is present elsewhere in the collection; in "A Few Words, A Little Shelter," for example, in "Of Men and Dogs," and in "Flaneur," which invokes Walter Benjamin, its unapologetic celebrator. For example, in his voluminous *Arcades Project* (the underground Paris arcades were ideal for *flanerie*), Benjamin was, in J.M. Coetzee's words, committed to "a new way of writing about civilization, using its rubbish as materials rather than its artworks: history from below rather than from above...."

Like Bernard and Kafka and Beckett, Benjamin was a professional intellectual of high standing with a strong inclination toward the abject and untamed, if not toward the bestial as such; an inclination which was partially realized in his writings on Baudelaire, Brecht and the Paris arcades. All unfinished.

I have cited numerous writers, both precedents and contemporaries, because Bernard is a bookish man, a longtime professor of literature with broad cultural interests. Of course, one cannot overlook his formidable Mr. Hyde side. Still, Hyde and all, there is a genial, companionable aspect to these fictions. And by extension, there is the strong sense that the narrator, neurotic and introverted though he may be, is an amusing person with whom to commit *flanerie*; that is, have a coffee while walking aimlessly through the streets of SoHo, say, and south Greenwich Village.

What accounts for this paradoxical geniality is the undercurrent of softness, fellow feeling and compassion in the texts. Although the narrator's obsessions are everywhere evident, the egocentrism is always modified by comical self-abnegation and irony. One feels a similar comradeship with Beckett for similar reasons.

To mention Beckett and Bernard side-by-side is not in any

way to diminish the younger of the pair. Which itself is a measure of the overall excellence of *The Man in the Stretcher*.

Harold Jaffe

# ABOUT THE AUTHOR

Kenneth Bernard is the author of nine previous books, including the book-length poem *The Baboon in the Nightclub*, the novel *From the District File*, and *Clown at Wall: A Kenneth Bernard Reader*. Long associated with John Vaccaro's Playhouse of the Ridiculous, Bernard has been producing work in three genres continuously for four decades and has received Guggenheim, Rockefeller, NEA, NEH, NY Creative Artists Public Service, and New York Foundation for the Arts grants. The stories in this collection originally appeared in some twenty different literary magazines, including *Paris Review, New American Review, Fiction International, Salmagundi, Frank, Harper's, Iowa Review, Triquarterly,* and *Confrontation*. Born in Brooklyn, raised in Massachusetts, Bernard has lived his entire adult life in New York City.

## Also from Starcherone Books

Theodore Pelton, *Endorsed by Jack Chapeau*, $7.95

Raymond Federman, *The Voice in the Closet*, $9

Nicolette de Csipkay, *Black Umbrella Stories*, $15

Aimee Parkison, *Woman with Dark Horses*, $16
WINNER OF THE 2003-04 STARCHERONE FICTION PRIZE

Raymond Federman, *My Body in Nine Parts*, $16
(forthcoming May 2005)

Nina Shope, *Hangings: Three Novellas*, $16
WINNER OF THE 2004-05 STARCHERONE FICTION PRIZE
(forthcoming July 2005)

Jeffrey DeShell, *Peter: An (A)Historical Romance*, $18
(forthcoming October 2005)

Order by mail with $2 s/h per book at Starcherone Books, PO Box 303, Buffalo, NY 14201, via the internet, www.starcherone.com, through our secure-channel link with PayPal, or through your local bookseller.